HORIZON STRIFE

Horizon Crossover Series (Book II)

by

Lyndi Alexander

Science Fiction novel from
Dragonfly Publishing, Inc.
www.dragonflypubs.com

HORIZON STRIFE

Horizon Crossover Series (Book II)
Science Fiction Novel

Paperback Edition
EAN 978-1-936381-73-9
ISBN 1-936381-73-7

Story Text Copyright ©2014 Barbara Mountjoy
Cover Art Copyright ©2014 Terri L. Branson
Dragonfly Logo Copyright ©2001 Terri L. Branson

Published in the United States of America by
Dragonfly Publishing, Inc.
Website: www.dragonflypubs.com

Horizon Crossover Series

HORIZON SHIFT
[Book I]

HORIZON STRIFE
[Book II]

HORIZON DYNASTY
[Book III]

ACKNOWLEDGMENTS

Thanks to my beta readers, Hank Henley, and E, who brought Temms Rogers to life from the very beginning.

I also appreciate the comments and letters of those who are reading the series. Your support really inspires me to keep it going!

Thank you to Terri Branson, who is more than just my publisher, but also a fan of these stories and their motley crew of characters. Thanks for sharing my vision and letting me share it with the world.

DEDICATION

For all those who challenge authority when it's wrong and who try to make the worlds better places to live.

PROLOGUE

THE door opened and slammed into the wall with a hollow metal *clang*.

Two men, blindfolded and bound, were shoved inside, bouncing off the hallway's narrow walls.

"Keep moving!" barked the gruff man who had brought them. He planted a hand firmly in the broad back of the captain of the mercenary ship *Ramman,* and then pushed him ahead into the darkness.

Behind him, his second-in-command grunted, his footsteps in an odd rhythm, as if he had tripped. He stumbled forward and bumped into the first man.

"Captain, what do they want?" he gasped between clenched teeth.

"Shut up," was the reply.

Captain Jak Moster had been a citizen of this corner of the cosmos for nearly sixty-five annuals. Forty of them he had spent dealing with the financial monster called the Agency that regulated business in the interplanetary space that contained planets Marriel and Terza, setting tariffs, laying down the rules, stealing whatever new technologies served their needs. The local governments couldn't or wouldn't take action against them.

Which meant that, right now, Jak and Ral were pretty much on their own.

Jak had a fairly good idea what was wanted here. His priority was to stay alive through this encounter. It could happen.

It might.

Sounds ahead indicated others waiting for their arrival, three separate voices engaged in conversation. At least one had heavy-heeled boots. That thought sent shudders through his knees. He had seen what a man who worked for the Agency had done to his former captain years before, with boots just like that. The captain hadn't survived.

Have I reached the end of the line?

He struggled to remain upright as they approached the others, the bit of light seeping in around the edges of the cloth blindfold letting him know it was a large room of some sort. Traces of tabac smoke lingered in the air, mixing with high-priced aftershave. A heavy hand grabbed his shoulder and slammed him into a hard wooden chair, jarring his spine. A shocked yell by his first officer Ral and simultaneous thump indicated the same treatment.

"Who are you working for?" a gravelly male voice demanded.

"Been working for myself, boss," Jak replied, his thick throat tight.

"Is that so?"

Movement in front of him, but no one touched him.

"It is."

Jak tried to balance firm commitment with a helping of respect, without sounding obsequious. Agents didn't take well to simpering sycophants. They were businessmen, not politicians.

"You received our new rate chart, didn't you?"

If only he could see them. He would know where the fist would come from. His stomach tensed in anticipation.

"Yes, sir, I did. I sent along what you asked for from the last two runs."

A hesitation.

"They were late."

"Boss, they were sent upon our arrival! Not our fault we got hung up at Havrila."

"Havrila. Yes. You did stop there for some time."

Silence.

What did they want?

"Any particular reason you stopped there? That port wasn't one of the original logbook entries."

That was it.

His heart sank. If they knew he had stopped at Havrila, they would suspect he had attended the meet-up with other captains planning to protest the Agency's control. Practically an act of treason. His mouth dried up and he couldn't form an answer.

"Well?" A hand passed close to his arm.

He couldn't reply. A vision of his wife holding their grandchild flashed before his eyes.

"How about you? Do you remember why your captain stayed so long?"

A loud thwack echoed in the room, followed by a yell of agony.

"My leg, my leg," Ral moaned.

Jak's blindfold was suddenly torn away, along with a handful of his abundant chestnut hair. The pain spread along the left side of his head like a slow-blooming fire. A quick glance showed him blood gushing from Ral's right leg, eviscerated almost to the bone, a matching red smear on a thick, nail-studded piece of wood a meter long held by a dark-suited man standing in front of him.

They were in some poorly-lit back room, not an Agency office. No, those were always spit-and-polish clean, as if Agents were some sort of nobility. They aspired to be that good. But then they had their not-so-pretty ways of doing things. A couple dusty wooden tables, these hard chairs, and a bottle of cheap booze on the sideboard. This spoke mercenary. Men who were unaccountable to anyone for their actions.

Which meant Jak and Ral were in even worse trouble.

"So, Moster, still finding an explanation hard to concoct? How about the truth?"

His questioner was a tall, dark-skinned man wearing a bulky black jacket. When the front of it swung open, Jak spied a projectile weapon in a leather holster. If his hands were free, he could get to it. He had to stall.

What could he say that didn't damn the rest of the conspirators?

Movement caught his eye but not in time to evade as the bloody piece of wood came in his direction, and then smashed into his right shoulder. Bone shattered in a crunch of misery. A nerve twitched, shooting pain down through his fingertips, and then his arm went numb. He tried not to show emotion, but a whimper crawled from between his dry lips.

"I paid my money," he whispered.

"What were you doing in Havrila?"

The wood raised up in the air just long enough to launch itself at Ral's leg again. A snap. Then his ankle hung at an odd angle. Ral gurgled in pain, rolling back and forth on the chair, but a lean, pale-eyed merc with a grungy beard held him in the seat. Ral's eyes were wild and frightened. Perhaps he'd guessed the information the Agent wanted.

"Who did you meet there? Did you discuss the location of the Ancients' base?"

That question surprised him, shaking Jak's firm mind-set. His shoulder fell, sending a hot wave of pain all the way to his fingertips. Was the question of unpaid tariffs a distraction? Or was this? Were they trying to trick him?

"That base is just a myth. No one's ever found it."

The man growled and backhanded him across the face. "Don't lie! We know some of the captains use the base. We must gain access."

Confusion battled pain. Why would the Agents be chasing old legends? What could they possibly gain seeking an imaginary station supposedly built by those who came long ago?

"I don't know anything of any base, except for those old stories. I swear on my life!"

"This is no game, Moster. We will find out which captains are using it, and we will destroy them. All of them. I'm giving you a chance to save your worthless life and that of your first mate here. Assuming you find him useful."

The dark-skinned man raised his hand, and the other man lifted the wood, preparatory to another strike. Jak choked over his words, forcing out some obsequious protest that he remained loyal, that he didn't deserve such treatment. It didn't matter.

The club fell on his other shoulder, splitting the skin open, and then onto his knee. Agony shot through him like a spray of meteors. He barely caught his breath before a frontal blow broke most of his ribs. Pain racked his midsection. A stray thought that bits of his ribs had penetrated the rest of his organs flashed in his mind like a trail of gray smoke. If someone hadn't had his collar, he would have melted to the floor.

"What about you, Ral? Ready for your medicine?"

His consciousness and his existence quickly fading, Jak heard another mighty thwack. Ral shouted in pain, and then spilled his ragged confession.

"Rogers! He was looking for artifacts to repair his ship. You want Temms Rogers!"

After that, the buzz of blood in Jak's ears roared so loud he heard nothing more.

CHAPTER 1

ONE thing Temms Rogers knew for sure, he had no time for a wife.

Captaining the former Confederation ship *Doubtful* swallowed all his time, his crew at full muster, thirty-eight members, and his schedule set with cargo transport jobs to keep them fed. They had come a long way during the past cycle of the sun, but they weren't free and clear yet.

Besides, he had a wife once.

Connie had taken everything but his son Tommy, his ship, and his soul when they had gone before the magistrate. He had kept all those things when the ship had crossed into this new universe through an alien wormhole. He meant to hang on to them.

The middle-aged captain stretched, his comfortable, well-worn chair sliding back from the desk in his bookcase-lined office near the command center of the *Doubtful*. His cup was empty. He needed more stimulants if he was going to contend with the pile of work on the smooth black plaz surface before he fell into bed at the end of the watch.

Which brought him back to the note on the top of the pile.

Temms, come down to the infirmary and see me when you're done for the night. I've got a surprise for you.

The note was signed with a capital O and two small hearts.

He had a pretty good idea what the surprise would be.

The thought sent a sick, guilty twinge spiraling through his gut. Stars forgive him, he had been lonely, and Okalani Boro had been more than accommodating. Since he rescued the runaway bride-to-be from her wealthy fiancé, she had encouraged Temms' interest. A beautiful woman, her heart was as big as the star system in which they found themselves. A valuable member of his crew, she had smoothly stepped into the shoes of the doctor they had lost, and she worked as hard as anyone on the ship.

She deserves better than me. At least someone who can devote the time to her needs. I've got thirty-seven other people who depend on me day and night. I can't be that man.

He let his loneliness drive him into her arms more frequently than he should have. She would have been satisfied to make it a permanent commitment. He knew that well enough. His conscience ate at him. He had used her.

It wasn't like that. We're both adults, and we enjoyed each other. She understood we acted in the moment, without strings.

Perhaps she did. She persisted, though, and that unsettled him. He had to break it off.

He just didn't know how.

This wasn't the time to deal with it. Some of the problems on his desk just couldn't wait. Lives depended on it. Dark clouds waited on their horizon. Trouble was coming.

He grabbed his cup, and then walked over to the small wooden cabinet that held his collection of fine teas he had collected through the last several voyages. Some of them had even survived the crossing through the wormhole nearly a year before, but those were few. Those he rationed, preserving that small link to home. For his work tonight, he chose a heavily spiced local blend with extra stims that would give him a solid kick in the hind end and several hours before he would get sleepy. He needed it.

He hardly filled the cup with hot water before a knock came at the door.

Another delay. He sighed. "Come in."

His son Tommy opened the door, hesitating before he entered. He wore his off-duty dungarees with a dark green pullover shirt. The kid was handsome, tall and blond with Temms' own pale blue eyes. *Chip off the old block*, the captain thought with not a little irony. At least there was something in his life he had done right.

Tommy's smile was a fraction of its usual brilliance as he studied Temms. "You sure?"

Temms set his tea aside and crossed to give his son a hug. "You know you're welcome any time."

The kid grinned and gave his father a manly pat on the back. "Great."

Why did Temms still think of him as a kid? He had nearly twenty annuals under his belt. Back home, he would be gunning for his own command by now. *He'll always be a little boy to me.*

"Want some tea?"

Tommy made a disgusted face at the tin Temms held out. "That twiggy stuff that Liang gave you? It tastes like unwashed socks."

"She promises me it contributes to health. Her mother gave it to her every day to boost her immune system."

"Healthy herbs and berries. Maybe dead animal skeletons. Eye of newt and all that. Delicious." The distinct wrinkling of his nose revealed his level of sarcasm. "That's all you have, Dad?"

"Of course not." He chuckled. Not for a moment had he expected Tommy to accept the offer. They had come to know each other pretty well since the crossover. "I've got some of that stim juice you like in the box."

"Now you're talking."

Tommy detoured on his way to the desk and grabbed the drink, and then plopped into one of the side chairs. "You're working late."

"Not by choice. I slacked off a couple shifts, but I won the ship's vector competition."

"That's my old man." Tommy laughed. "Well done."

Temms crossed slowly to his desk chair, basking in the comfort of rare private time with his son. So many demands separated them, even working on the same ship. They managed to grab a meal together once or twice a week, which was more than they had back on Gilada, when he had been out on missions and Tommy had been finishing up classes at the Confederation school.

So this is progress, right?

He took his chair and sipped his tea while sizing up his son's demeanor. Tommy's smile had faded. Not good. "So this isn't just a personal visit. What's up?"

Tommy leaned forward, his elbows on the desk, his gaze intense. "Tas intercepted several comm messages. The Agency's tracing us."

An angry flush rose through the captain's rib cage. "They're what?"

"At least four separate episodes just today. Guess you really set someone's tail on fire with that last announcement. I'd suggest you change the location of your scheduled meeting coming up at Roandock. Otherwise you're likely to have some uninvited guests."

Suggestion: Temm's face twisted in a scowl as he leaned back in his chair, his fingers tightening around his cup. "These bastards just keep pushing! After what happened to Jak Moster when he refused to pay the Agency their blood money—"

"And it'll happen to you, too, Dad, if you don't back off." Tommy's gaze was troubled. "They've established their domain in this universe for thirty annuals or more before we came here. You aren't going to stop them."

"Not by myself. That's why I called this meeting. If the sector's captains for hire band together, we should be able to effect change." He frowned. "Just because something has limped into a lame tradition doesn't make it right. The Agency skims the cream off every deal that takes place in this sector, and provides nothing in return. You saw that latest demand. An additional ten percent! There's no reason we should give up our profits to fatten their purses."

Temms couldn't understand why some of the other captains weren't as outraged as he over the Agency's petty controls. Old Lestand explained it as a cost of doing business: "You know what's coming. Bend over and take it. Then charge your customer enough to cover the cost of the hemorrhoid surgery."

Temms couldn't buy that. It was wrong. He championed free enterprise. It was how he earned his living in the new universe, after all. But for an organization to exist by extorting honest businessmen, while contributing no value in return, was bloodsucking leechery at its very worst. He had no respect for that.

"Look, I get the outrage, and I know you're only looking out for your people, D—Captain. But the Agency doesn't mess around. Moster's ship is not the only one to be hit this rotation. Ships that don't work with them tend to disappear, or at least their captains do. Moster's missing, his second in command lost a leg trying to save his captain, from his report. Do you want to see something happen to Liang?"

"Of course not." Temms lips set tight against each other, like bricks in a dividing wall, sealing his resolve. His young navigator-turned-first officer was hardly defenseless. "It won't come to that. When they comprehend that all the captains are united against them, they'll have to take note and change their policy."

"Oh they'll take note, all right."

Tommy got to his feet, his gaze serious. "Then they'll take names and yours will be right at the top of the list…with a big target over it."

Something cold snaked through Tommy's words and wrapped itself around the base of Temms' spine. He was likely correct. Temms wasn't only risking his ship, but he was putting his crew at risk, as well. Could he unilaterally make that decision for all of them?

Of course he could. He was the captain. That was his job.

Temms previously had been subject to the control of an organization, the Confederation, which had ordered him to take actions he knew were morally wrong. He had bucked that system and had prevented his commanders from taking over a planet that didn't want Confederation rule. When something was right, one just had to take a stand.

Despite some painful losses, they had survived that. They would survive this.

He put down his cup as he stood and made his way around the desk to give his son another hug. The human contact reassured him. "Thanks for looking out for all of us, Tom. I've heard what you have to say, and I've listened. Let me think about it." He stepped back and smiled.

Tommy rolled his eyes. "That always means you're going to do it anyway. You're just stalling me."

Temms chuckled. "Maybe. I'm a stubborn old bird."

His son didn't bend. His voice lowered, and emotion flooded it with warmth. "I don't want to see that bird cooked, Dad. The fact they're spying on us is damned unsettling. For all we know, they've got a ship off the starboard bow with their laser weapon trained on this desk."

He glanced at the port in the rear of the office as if he expected to see exactly that, and Temms couldn't help looking, too, even as he chided himself for the compulsion.

"I said I'll think about it. Now go on. I have a lot to do yet tonight." He gestured at the desktop, though he knew at this point he would likely not return to the stack. Instead, he would be puzzling through how to give the Agency a kick in the teeth without getting in harms' way. Quite a feat, if he could pull it off.

Tommy's mouth dropped open as if he was going to add something, but he shut it before anything escaped. His eye fell on Okalani's note, and his eyebrow crept upward. "You're going to the infirmary?"

Temms quickly swept the note into his top drawer. "I'm not."

Tommy laughed. "Might as well. She's a pretty woman, Dad, with one amazing warm heart. You need someone to love. It's been over a year now since Kitana died. It's time."

Maybe so, but none of your business, lad.

"Good night, Tommy," he said firmly.

The young man shook his head. "You're stubborn, all right. G'night, Dad."

Temms clapped his son on the shoulder and walked him to the door. "Better day tomorrow, right?"

"Sure, Dad." Tommy headed down the narrow hall without a look behind.

Temms wondered where he was going at this hour of the night, even as he conjectured possibilities, acknowledging it probably wasn't his business any more. The two of them had always butted heads, as fathers and sons tended to do, especially since Tommy had gotten old enough to express his interest in the Confederation school.

Connie hated the idea of Tommy following his father's footsteps, and Tommy loved using that against his mother. When he and Connie had separated, and Temms met Kitana, Tommy had used that relationship as a wedge between his father and himself.

Then the young man disguised his transfer to Temms' ship to spy out what kind of man his father really was, just before Temms and his colleagues rebelled against the immoral conduct of their Confederation superiors. He ended up on the far side of a wormhole, battered and bruised, and one of Temms' few remaining officers. Since then, they had bonded as father and son, but also as men who had been through combat side-by-side.

That meant Tommy was a man, just like any member of the crew, who had the right to his privacy and his own secrets. His dad didn't get to pry any more.

That might be just fine by me. Got enough on my to-do list.

Temms sighed and returned to his desk, eyeing the pile of work. After his talk with Tommy he wasn't going to be good company for anyone, especially Okalani. He sent her a comm message, text only, that indicated he would be working late and not to expect him. Then he settled in to make that promise a reality.

Tomorrow would be a better day.

CHAPTER 2

SITTING at the cleared-off desk in the infirmary, Okalani Boro read the message from the captain and choked down her disappointment, putting on a smile instead.

Temms was a good man. He worked hard to assure his crew had everything, denying himself personal satisfaction in order to finish his tasks instead.

He had certainly provided her a home just when she needed it.

What would life have been like if she had really married that insufferable prig Geoffrey? She would likely have had all the comforts life could offer, since he had piles of old family money and a fancy title that continued to bring him more to go with it.

But his favorite occupation had been telling her how stupid she was. That she would never be useful. That she would never be a doctor. That she would never be anything.

Who needed that?

She had made the impulsive decision to break it off with Geoffrey on the tarmac as they were heading to their big, fancy wedding. Then she had landed literally in Temms Rogers' arms. Geoffrey had even punched the captain in his bid to recover his property.

The memory brought her a soft laugh.

"He never exerted himself that much physically the whole time I knew him," she murmured. The grand show certainly hadn't changed her mind. All it had done was reassure Okalani she was making the right choice, and Temms more determined to secure her on his ship.

The *Doubtful* already had Dr. Montgomery, but the spry, older man was more than happy to teach her what he knew. He had been killed in action, and Okalani received a sudden promotion to chief medical officer.

She hoped she had been successful in her professional duties.

She had certainly been less so in her personal life.

Since his initial, impulsive gesture to rescue her, she had had a special place for Temms Rogers in her heart that had grown into real love. She admired everything about him, even his flaws. She had watched him struggle with his relationship with his son, and perhaps overcome the rifts that had separated them years before. It was hard to tell from day to day. They still butted heads on a regular basis.

But she always hoped that someday he would ask her to be his wife.

He still could. She just needed to be patient. Or maybe brave enough to ask him.

Maybe someday.

Her plan for the evening squashed, she sighed and turned off her monitor.

The infirmary echoed with the quiet, lit only by the small lamp on her neatly-cleared desk. The main room was small, compared to the treatment areas in most of the hospitals where she had trained, five by seven meters, with white walls and a green lino floor. The lab and an extra multi-purpose room lay off to the right, through a short hallway. She had been fortunate not to need more space while she treated the usual string of work-related injuries that passes through her doors. Because storage was at a premium, as it was on most ships, she had wrangled every spare inch she could with glass-doored cabinetry, two walls' worth, floor to ceiling, keeping her medical equipment for easy access. It was her space. She wouldn't trade it for all the worlds.

In the meantime, she faced another night alone.

"That was your choice, Lani," she scolded herself. "You could have had Geoffrey."

She clicked off the infirmary lights and closed up for the day, making her way to her room on the deck below.

Her quarters were inherited from the former doctor, two rooms, each about three by four meters, along with a necessary. As a senior officer, she was also privileged to have a small port where she could look out at the stars. Her rooms were located, as were most of the crew quarters, on the second of four decks.

The top deck held the command offices, including her medical suite. Engineering consumed most of the third deck, with the remainder of the crew quarters fit in around the outside, mostly assigned to the engineering staff, since they seemed to like the lullaby of their droning engine sounds. The lowest deck carried cargo and housed their Bellonan security team, a mated pair of shape-shifting aliens.

For the first time in her life, she had the chance to decorate her living area exactly as she wanted it. No sisters cluttering up her table with dirty laundry. No intimate grunts of sexual pleasure between roommates and their clandestine overnight partners. No Geoffrey. Just her.

As a result, the walls held a mishmash of eclectic choices, paintings, hangings, and floral wreaths in a multitude of colors and shapes. Whenever she found something she loved on their travels through the Marriel system, she brought it back to help create her space. And she loved it here.

Only one thing she could add that would make her happier.

Before she could get lost along that frustrating trail of thought, her comm buzzed. Releasing her disappointment, she answered it. "Dr. Boro."

At first, all she heard was wheezing.

"Okalani," came a tortured voice. "Need—help."

Her trained ear recognized the signs of respiratory distress. She tapped the comm once more to identify the speaker. Riviera Brown, chief science officer. "What's wrong? Something with the hydroponics? Where are you?"

The only response she received was a shuddering gasp. This would require hands-on. The ship wasn't so large she couldn't ascertain Riviera's whereabouts. "I'm on my way!"

Where would she find the woman?

This hour of the night, she would likely be off-duty. If not, the doctor could proceed to the science section above. Okalani grabbed her medical kit and took off at a run down the corridor outside her quarters, halfway around the deck to Riviera's quarters, finding the door unlocked. It swung open at her touch. The large, dark-skinned woman lay in her pajamas on her disheveled bed, struggling for each breath.

"Stars preserve us," Okalani whispered. She hurried to Riviera's side and scanned her, finding her breathing labored and her heart struggling to keep up with the reduced oxygen levels. First order of treatment was the administration of epinephrine to stimulate her respiratory system. She did that, and then stepped back a moment.

"What did you get into, honey?"

"Don't—know," Riviera gasped. "Been here—since I got off duty."

The doctor glanced around the small, single room for a clue, flipping on the overhead light to help her search. Her theory was that it had to be something nearby. As constricted as Riviera was, Okalani supposed this affliction had come on quickly. If she had waited much longer to call for help, she might have been dead.

Nothing readily presented itself. These quarters had a definite "lived-in" look, worn clothing piled on the floor, a few books scattered across a small table, a stack of data pads on the small dresser next to the bed. But nothing that seemed primed to induce anaphylaxis.

Waiting for her patient's breathing to ease, Okalani continued her scanning, finding she had a fever in addition to the elevated heart rate. Either of those symptoms might happen as a result of hyperventilation, but the doctor's gut told her that wasn't the case. Something else was at work here.

"Tell me what you've done since shift change."

Between long, wheezing breaths, Riviera forced out a reply. "Went by the galley. Brought back some greens for dinner. Then filed some reports."

The big woman labored to sit upright. Okalani helped her untangle her legs from her white sheets, noting the discomfort of Riviera's skin, so hot to the touch. She scanned her again to assess the progress of the medication, and then caught a glimpse of a bright scarlet, patterned rash on the back of Riviera's neck. She had never seen anything like it before.

"Honey, can you take off your top, please?"

She walked around the bed to the other side, where she could get a better view, and took a small, handheld light from her kit.

Riviera looked like she would protest at first. But, wearily, she shrugged off her shirt and dropped it on the floor. Examination showed the rash continued down her back and around her rib cage, fading into her dark skin at her waistline.

"How long have you had this rash?"

Riviera uttered a short gasp. "Didn't know I had one."

How could she not know? It looked painful, or at least like it should itch. "Really?" Okalani reached in her kit for some protective gloves. "Have you been working with anything new or particularly allergenic?"

"Nothing." She fought to catch her breath. "What's wrong with me?"

"Wish I knew."

Okalani ran her fingers over the rash, finding it firm, dry, and raised. After she examined the swath across the woman's shoulders, Okalani was startled to find that the rash now extended further, wrapping around toward her throat. How could it spread that fast?

"I'd better get you to the infirmary," she said. She called for her corpsman, Lavan, to bring the transport gurney down to Riviera's quarters. "Was anyone working with you during your watch? I'll want to check them out too."

"Shiro there. Earlier." Riviera broke into a coughing fit and didn't add anything else. Okalani braced her upright with her own body, the violent coughs threatening to send them both onto the floor.

Sympathetic to the woman's discomfort, Okalani's mind whirled through the possibilities. Hopefully this was a one-person affliction, anaphylaxis of some sort. A few hours in the infirmary, a soothing cream and some assistance clearing her patient's lungs of whatever affected them, and that would be it.

She wanted to leave it there, but she couldn't. It might have been the greens she ate for dinner, or something more insidious. Perhaps it was a plant-based infection triggered by a sample in her hydroponics work or a science department investigation. Riviera and maybe one or two others would be affected, whoever had direct contact with the irritating substance.

Whatever had given Riviera the symptoms might spread though the ventilation system, if it was pollen-borne or otherwise transmissible. Then it might afflict everyone ship-wide.

It could get very, very bad. Quickly.

Panic flaring, she fought it back. She debated calling the captain, but didn't want to bother him unless she had to. He had said he was busy, after all. Time enough to let him know, once she determined whether it was a crisis or an isolated incident.

It might be a good excuse just to touch base with him, after all. They would have no time to cuddle while she had patients in the infirmary, but maybe just seeing him would be enough to fulfill her emotional need for reassurance.

As long as it was nothing serious.

Her corpsman arrived, his brown eyes still puffy from sleep. "What's going on?" he asked.

"Respiratory distress and a rash and fever. Maybe something from the lab."

He smiled at Riviera. "Don't worry. The Doc'll have you cured in no time."

The still-wheezing Riviera managed a nod. His gentle hands quickly set up the folded gurney he had carried down, and they helped their patient onto it, along with the remains of her dinner in a medical sample bag. She was a big woman, and negotiating the corners with the gurney proved a little tricky, but they made it to the infirmary fairly quickly.

Lavan inserted an intravenous line and set out the cardio-respiratory monitor for Okalani to attach. No blockage showed up on the monitor, but the fluid level in her lungs was a bit more than it should be. Riviera's breathing hadn't improved much, so the doctor gave her an additional dose of medicine.

"Standard blood draw for now. I'm going to have to keep an eye on her for awhile before I decide what else to do."

"If it's a contaminant, it should pass from her system before long," he suggested, his voice a warm tenor, as always calm and even-toned. It took a lot to rattle this one. "I can run some scans on her meal, too."

"Agreed." And if it wasn't? She didn't want to think about that just yet. "Call Shiro Vered down. She worked in the lab today, too."

"Yes, doctor."

She made sure Riviera was as comfortable as possible, and then left Lavan to his work. It shouldn't take long to determine what she was up against, at least separate it between allergen or infection. Then if she had to, she would give the captain a call and add to that huge pile she knew he had on his desk. Another wedge in the possibilities between them. But this was her job and that was his, so it was just the way things had to be.

CHAPTER 3

THE captain's room was dark and silent, when he was disturbed from his fitful sleep by a faint light in the far corner.

It pulsed there, almost as if breathing. Then expanded slowly.

By the time he was awake enough to focus on it, the golden light had grown to nearly the size of a man, though it remained a nebulous cloud with a vague shadow of a human form within.

"What the—" He scrambled upright, hand reaching for his comm to call security.

Captain Temms Rogers, we shall not bring you harm. Do not be afraid.

The voice resonated in his head, a familiar one, that of Captain Benjamin, one of his instructors at the Confederation school. He was a universe away from the Confederation. But that same voice had come to him a year ago when the Ancients' machine had activated, just before the miracle that had saved his ship from Burko for the second time. Though others present in the room had been addressed in the voices of persons they knew and respected from their own pasts, Temms had been reassured by the voice of his flight instructor to whom he owed much of his professional skill.

Yes, you have guessed our identity. When we touched your mind at that moment of crisis in your life, we formed a bond. We were able to find you again. It is now our time of need, and we must ask your assistance.

The Ancients, who were so far ahead of his petty mechanical skills and abilities, needed *his* help? It seemed a little improbable.

"You are in crisis?"

As you say. We have lost something very important, just as we were about to share something wonderful with your people. You can help us locate it.

Temms rubbed his tired eyes as he sat on the edge of his bed. "Sure. We can do that. You've helped us when we needed it most. What are you looking for?"

He reached for a datapad and stylus to take notes.

Something has been stolen from our physical plant in the star system. A control device that will allow us to intermingle with you, to teach you, to help all our children take greater steps toward growth and power.

"Who has it?"

We do not know. Just that it is gone. We have faith that you can find it, Captain Temms Rogers. Your heart is brave, your will is strong.

Flattering, but he didn't have the first idea where to even begin looking. "Where is this plant? We'll need to gather clues, information."

A pause.

We must be cautious in revealing the plant's location. When it was once known, that is when it was attacked and the crucial element taken. We have searched for it without success. We believe it is being purposely concealed by those who wish us to fail."

Maybe he just wasn't fully awake yet, but the words echoed in his mind like the script of a bad detective holodrama. "So?"

We shall contact you again, when the time draws near. You will be well rewarded for your service, and receive all that you deserve.

Well, there. That was something that sounded more concrete and encouraging. Temms very seldom turned down work that paid. "We could use some healthy rewards. Thank you for your confidence in us."

He waited for a reply, but nothing came. The vision slowly dissipated, and it was dark once again. He yawned and stretched and looked at the clock. It certainly wasn't time for his morning shift yet. He maneuvered back onto his rack, trying to get comfortable again.

He had just drifted into light sleep when he was dragged back to consciousness by the persistent buzzing of his captain's comm.

"It's a crisis already?" he mumbled, half-awake.

"Captain, it's Okalani. I'm so sorry to bother you, but I need you in the infirmary."

His brain struggled to grasp the switch in speaker. Hadn't he told her he couldn't meet her? What in the hells time was it? "Now?"

"It's an emergency."

He twisted to peer at his monitor for the time. Halfway through third turn. Not a casual call at all. He groaned and sat up. "On my way."

He punched the comm to silence and stood, his bones cracking.

Damn it all, I might be pushing the far edge of the first half of my lifespan, but it was only the first half! I shouldn't be disintegrating yet.

He donned his pants, and then grabbed whatever bright-colored tropical print shirt he had been wearing earlier, shrugging it on as he headed for the infirmary. The movement kicked his brain and body into better synch.

"Emergency?" *Huh.*

If it needed the captain's presence, that meant it was likely something bad. He hated when it was something bad. Maybe it was something as simple as Tommy getting into a fight down in the exercise suite and Okalani had called him because she knew he would want to know.

Straightening his shoulders, he pushed through the doorway to medical. "All right, I'm here. What is it?"

His first glance took in the doctor without her usual lab coat, her hair down around her shoulders. His second glance found science officer Riviera Brown lying on one of the beds, her dark skin flushed, an oxygen mask on her face. Engineer Dani Jamar, her usual cheery smile missing, sat on the bed next to Riviera's, breathing with some effort. One of the corpsmen moved about them, equipment in hand.

"D, what's the matter?"

Dani tried to speak, but finally just waved at him.

Okalani came to meet him, her hand on his arm holding him back. "Don't get too close to them yet. I'm still testing."

Why was she worried if he got too close? "Why are they here? And are they contagious?"

"Riviera called, in severe respiratory distress. By the time we got her breathing under control, Dani showed up here, headed along the same path."

Temms frowned. The two women didn't work together, and as far as he knew, they didn't socialize much. Hells, Brown didn't socialize with anyone. The woman stood nearly two meters tall when her hair was all kinked out. A real imposing figure. She spent most of her time alone. Dani, now, was much more the mingling type, a bright light on his staff.

"Something in the air?"

"We're trying to determine that." The doctor gestured toward the back rooms, where two others worked at microscopes and other apparatus. "It's a sudden-onset problem, and they weren't together. No one else took sick, either in engineering or the science department. If it was something in the air—" She shook her head. "I'm sorry I don't have more information for you."

Dani began to gasp for air, the effort shaking her slender frame. Okalani hurried to help her lie down, strapping an oxygen mask to her face.

Temms felt extraneous and helpless. "What do you need me to do?" he asked.

"I'm not sure you can do anything," she said, continuing her ministrations. "I was a little worried about calling you down here, in case you'd be affected." She hesitated and eyed the captain.

Again with that reference. "Why would I be affected?"

She opened her mouth to answer, and then closed it and shook her head. "Just a theory. Nothing positive. It's—anyway, I knew you'd want to see for yourself."

If he had been more awake, he might have pressed her, but it didn't seem like an important point. She seemed to have everything under control. Handling two sick people should be well within her capacity as chief medical officer.

Feeling tension set in, he rolled his shoulders. "I'll leave you to it, then. If they need anything, notify me. I'll assign crew to cover their watches."

Dani wheezed her thanks. Riviera didn't respond and appeared to be asleep. Maybe that was her best hope to be back on her feet soon.

"If anything changes, don't hesitate to call me. Do you need anything else? More people?"

"If I do, I know where to find them. Thanks, Temms." She shooed him with her gloved hands and went back to her work.

He returned to his quarters, but try as he might, he couldn't find his way back to sleep. A rueful recollection of his cadet days flitted through his mind, when he could fall asleep in the time it took to close his eyes, anytime, anywhere.

I'm getting to be an old man.

If they had remained in the original universe, he would have been scheduled to retire from Confederation service in another seven years. He would likely have remained for another ten, just because he was a single man with grown children. What else was there to do for the last thirty or more years of his life?

But after he had passed through an alien wormhole, he and the few survivors of his original crew found themselves in a new place where retirement was the last option for him. Everything they had built before was gone.

He had recruited new crew and started on a life as a mercenary. His ship was for hire to transport cargo, provide security, whatever people needed. He would be working probably the rest of his life.

That suited him.

His crew had been his family for a long time. Even if the papers severing his ties to Connie had been finalized six years before, he had spent whole chunks of time away from home on Confederation service. Dani and Riviera and the others had been his world, his foundation, those he could count on. He had taken on officers that no other captain could deal with, and he had built himself a family.

And he didn't need his family down sick.

With a frustrated rumble, he tapped out orders on his computer, calling up second in line in science and engineering watch lists, with a minimal explanation that the firsts were in the infirmary and they needed to show up first thing at dayturn.

That done, he pushed back his chair and stood. As much as he needed more sleep, he knew it was unlikely. Might as well surrender to the inevitable.

He stepped into his shower, making a quick pass at refreshing himself, and then put on black pants and a particular bright shirt with red and peach-colored flowers. Though the supply room had been stocked with ample numbers of Confederation uniforms after the crossover, he didn't require anyone to wear them. He preferred his loud, comfortable shirts. They made him feel confident. Straightening the shirttails, he grabbed his comm unit and headed up to the bridge.

* * *

WHEN he stepped onto the gray-carpeted command center of his ship, the half-staffed night watch purred along like the well-oiled machine it was.

The six-seater bridge, some ten meters square, easily accommodated the exchange of information among those manning its posts. It being third-turn, one officer covered nav and tactical, another monitored the comm console and a third kept track of the science and engineering readings.

Liang Chao Chen sat in the captain's chair in the center of the back row of seats, feet tucked under her, reading something on her monitor. As first officer, the petite, almond-eyed woman had things well under her control. Her maturity and management skills often made Temms forget she was just eighteen, a year younger than Tommy.

"Captain?" Liang uncurled her body and got to her feet. "Is something wrong?"

"Couldn't sleep." He waved at the chair. "As you were."

She still didn't sit. Instead, she studied him. As usual, her instincts were excellent. "No, something troubles you."

He chuckled. "When does something not trouble me, Liang?" He crossed to an empty station and accessed ship's reports.

She glanced at the other three officers on the bridge, and then crossed to stand next to Temms, speaking so only he could hear. "You take your responsibilities as Captain seriously. I know this. It sets you apart from my previous captain."

Temms rolled his eyes. "Really? That's all that sets me apart? He sold you into slavery to pay his bills, Liang. I think I've got a few more points on him than just working hard."

She smiled at last. "Perhaps."

"Perhaps." He snorted. The reports scrolled on the monitor, and he scanned each of them, looking for anything that seemed disquieting. The situation with the Agency had reached a head, there was no question. The fact they were monitoring the *Doubtful* so closely probably meant they knew of Temms' quiet rabblerousing among the other captains, looking for sympathetic souls.

Not a good sign.

Her sharp gaze fastened on the information scrolling up the monitor. "I warned you this would happen."

He nodded. "You did." He snapped the screen off and turned to face her. "But how long are we expected to let these people bully us into submission? Someone has to take a stand."

She crossed her arms, looking up into his eyes. Even though she barely came up to his shoulder, she made her presence felt as if she were his height or more. "You have other avenues."

He cocked a brow. "Which avenues are those, Liang?"

She took a deep breath. "You performed a great service for the Consortium on Perpetra. The Prince told you he was in your debt. Their financial empire is one of the few that has successfully challenged the Agency."

"I know. But I don't want to call in those favors unless I have to. This ought to be something that a strong league of captains, allied like brothers, could handle."

He had thought of this solution many times, but always came back to the metaphor of the schoolyard bully. The victim could call the headmaster and have the offender disciplined, but once the punishment was complete, the bully reappeared on the playground, more determined than ever. No, this time the victims needed to stand up for themselves. Once and for all.

Persistent as usual, she opened her mouth to go on, but he held up a hand to cut her off. "I'm still thinking, Liang. I do have options. I just want to test some of them out before I settle for something I'm unhappy with." He let his hand drop onto her shoulder in a fatherly pat. "I heard you. Don't worry."

Her lips pursed with displeasure, but she nodded and stepped back.

"Is there anything else I can provide you, Captain? Any specific reports? Any action you wish me to take?"

"Just do what you've been doing, Liang. I'll let you know if there's something I need." He surveyed the night crew. "Anything I can do for you?"

Liang chewed her lip. Then looked away. "Get some rest. You're looking tired."

"Sounds like good advice. I'll take it. Good night, Liang."

She grunted and retook the captain's seat as he left the bridge. Feeling a little more upbeat, he decided his ship was in good hands for the night. Perhaps he would try to get some more sleep after all.

CHAPTER 4

WHEN the message buzzed into his comm, Benzi Quinn grunted and rolled over.

"Not my bloody shift. Not mine."

The buzzer continued on and off until he finally got up and slouched across the room to read it.

The third time the words finally sank in. Frustration chased them into his throat.

"What in Sprechan's name is the Cap thinking? I just got off." He eyed the clock. "Wasn't but half a shift."

But Rogers' order was an order.

A year or two before, prior to his service on the *Doubtful*, he might have ignored a directive he felt was unfair. He had lost several positions that way, and had come pretty close to hitting bottom. Rogers had taken him in when he probably shouldn't have, and he had earned Benzi's respect.

So I'm off to work. Hurrah.

Rubbing his thick black hair, matted from half a rough night's sleep, he lumbered into the necessary to empty his overfull bladder, giving himself a few minutes for his brain to catch up to working speed. When he walked back out, he glanced over at his adopted son's bed. It was empty.

Now where's that boy gone off to?

"Monty? Where are you, snapper?"

He listened for a moment, and then followed a faint scraping sound to the second room in his small quarters. Monty insisted on sleeping in the same room as Benzi, which meant the room assigned for his separate sleeping space could be transformed into a work area. A large wooden table centered the room, and Monty sat at its far side, a whole array of small metal parts spread out before him. He had created something that stood about a meter tall, intricately interwoven with metal clamps, joints and flat pieces. The boy continued to tinker with the structure, soldering pieces almost faster than Benzi could keep track.

It was ticking.

When Benzi realized the last, his stomach seized up.

"Snapper!" he barked, a little sharper than he meant to.

The boy dropped the soldering gun and froze, not looking in Benzi's direction, just staring off into midair.

The ticking went on.

Benzi growled and came around the table, laying a hand gently on the boy's shoulder, squelching the impulse to shake him back into awareness. The small movements and successes of construction soothed him. He had been instrumental in helping Benzi and the engineering staff build the alien device that had saved the *Doubtful* from destruction at the hands of Rogers' Confederation enemies, that was for sure.

The other thing that was for sure was that Monty bonded to Benzi and no one else. Their histories might have been similar. Benzi didn't know, as Monty didn't talk much, and certainly didn't share stories from his past. Dr. Okalani said the boy lived in his own world, spoke his own language, perhaps as the result of some kind of trauma. He reacted to sharp stimuli by pulling away and hiding, or just shutting down.

Like now.

"Snap. I'm not mad. Just worried. What's making that noise?"

He crouched down, trying to see inside the thing.

Like as not, lad wouldn't come up with anything dangerous. He's got no reason to hurt any of us. We're likely t'only ones who's treated him decent. Better than them stinkin' green aliens.

"Whatcha building, little man?"

He poked at the corners of the thing. The small parts were fastened in pretty closely, and he couldn't find a hole that passed all the way through. The ticking speeded up. His breath caught.

A frenetic whir came from inside the box, and the slight, brown-haired boy suddenly snapped to attention. His face lit with anticipation. "Here comes!"

Benzi couldn't help the wave of apprehension that ran through him. He pulled them both back from the table, ready to land on the boy if an explosion went off.

"Craw! Craw! Craw!"

The most unpleasant bird call Benzi had even heard assailed his ears, actually causing enough pain he had to cover them. It was halfway between piercing and shrieking with bass undertones that rattled his jaw. The noise continued for nearly thirty seconds before Monty tapped the top of the box and blessed quiet returned.

He looked up at Benzi with an angelic smile. "Pop get up now."

"Get up? What?"

"Pop get up. Time to work."

The room hadn't disintegrated, so Benzi pushed himself to his feet, a little sheepish. "So you're sayin' you made this so we'd get up for work?"

The boy nodded, his wide smile radiating delight. He put down his tools and ducked under Benzi's arm, skittering across to his dresser to yank out some mismatched separates. Babbling to himself in a singsong tone, he pulled his clothes on, oblivious to Benzi's discomfort.

"Sprechan's holy fires, I was never cut out to be a father," Benzi muttered. He studied the makeshift alarm clock a moment, allowing himself to take pride in the clever way the boy had cobbled together Benzi's discards to produce something useful. "We got to do something about that noise, though, Snap."

With a weary sigh, he grabbed his uniform and ducked into the necessary to take a quick shower. What would he do with Monty while he was on watch? He hadn't made arrangements, and it wasn't like he could do like his old da had always done, and send him out into the streets for the day. For one thing, they were cruising in space, a distinct lack of streets. And second, Monty just wasn't like any other child he had ever known.

For one thing, he didn't seem to care who was around him, particularly if he had a gadget to work on. He focused on tasks to the point of being oblivious to others, even those who might bother him. Once he had learned where everything was, he had become reasonably self-sufficient. He could feed himself a meal from Benzi's private stores, or find his way to the galley alone. He dressed himself, though not according to any style of fashion Benzi had ever seen. In all likelihood, Benzi could leave him in their shared quarters alone till shift's end, and he wouldn't necessarily come to harm.

But we could end up with something worse than that accursed alarm.

Supervision was better.

Benzi, half-dried off and in a hurry now, having dawdled over Monty's machine longer than he should have, tripped over several piles of their belongings on the floor as he tried to gather enough mostly-clean clothing to wear. Monty didn't always pick up whatever he used, and in fact, tended to drop whatever he was finished with right where he stood. Come to think of it, Benzi himself wasn't much better.

He shoved his legs into his work pants and shimmied into a plain blue shirt. Monty would have to go down to engineering with him. Even if Dani wasn't there, someone would help keep an eye on him. Maybe Liang had dug up some more of those alien artifacts that needed decoding. The kid was even good at translation.

But he don't have my special gift.

With a superior grin, Benzi leaned out to see what the boy was doing. "All right, Snapper. Let's gather a bag of tools. We're heading below."

The kid had beaten him to it. With a wide smile, he stood by the door with his tool belt fastened around his waist. "Waiting!" he chirped.

"You're something else, and that's no lie." He roughed up the boy's hair and then grabbed his own kit as they headed out the door for engineering.

CHAPTER 5

TEMMS paced in the parked shuttle for nearly half an hour before Tommy signaled that he was allowed to step foot on Marriel.

"About time," he muttered as he strode down the plank from the open hatch. The scent of wood smoke filled the air in this forested area outside of Roandock. The thought of convening their meeting at the bar of Oke Runyon, where he had first met Liang, had crossed his mind, but Runyon had betrayed him once. He wasn't stupid enough to give him a second chance. Roandock was a bigger city, with less chance that a group of ship captains getting together would be attention-grabbing.

Or so he hoped.

Veiled warnings received by two of the captains planning to attend the gathering had everyone on edge. He had given in to his security chief's demand that the three-mile area around the rental cabin and the attendees be thoroughly vetted by Tommy and Nim Williams before he walked in.

The Agency was that malicious.

Only he and his men knew of the silent, cloaked security team he had brought along as his last line of defense. They, too, had paced the perimeter of the lodge, making sure all was secure. Were such serious precautions necessary?

Everyone Temms had spoken with face to face seemed to be honest and invested in the cause.

But you could never be too careful.

C. T. Dutton waited for him just inside the door, his tall, lean body dressed in black head to toe, his olive-toned skin giving him the impression of a deep tan, his silver hair close-cropped in the military cut he still wore years after leaving the service. "Thought maybe you'd reconsidered. Or that your boy had."

"Pesky kids. You promote them to security chief, and suddenly they know everything," Temms growled. His eyes scanned the large wood-paneled room, noting the stuffed animal heads mounted along the front and back walls. The retreat appealed to the sportsman in him, the wallpaper in muted dark green, and the polished wooden floors giving a nod to the natural world. Several large tables formed a great square in the middle of the room, chairs lined up on the outside, facing in, in preparation for the meeting to come.

Tommy and Nim mingled with other security people from the attending crews. They hoped to gather information that would help in coordinating a strong resistance.

Temms checked his timepiece. Seventeen captains had agreed to participate. Thirteen were here. He had to wait a few minutes more.

"Hey, Tom's a good kid. Strong, like his old man." C. T. grinned and clapped him on the shoulder. "He'll be bucking for your seat before too long."

Temms laughed. "Hold on now. I've got a few more good years left in me, I think. Let's not rush the boy into that command chair."

The thought of Tommy, with his hot temper and random impulse control, in charge of the power of a spaceship gave him a little shiver.

Maybe someday. Maybe someday. Not just yet.

"Just an impression," the other said, laughing. "Don't think you need to worry today. Come on and say hello to Kyndra."

Temms walked with C. T. to greet the others, including C. T.'s longtime companion Kyndra Vilsin. The redhead studied him with eyes the color of chocolate drops.

"Still too tense," she said.

Temms shrugged. "The workload never seems to break down, Kyndra."

She trailed a finger along his arm, leaving a string of tingles. "You should find ways to relax." Her mind projected warm thoughts into his of a shadowy woman cuddled against him, no doubt what they were doing.

"Hey!" He jerked back from her. Embarrassed, he covered with a forced chuckle. "No fair."

She only chuckled softly, taking C. T.'s arm.

Empaths. So glad I don't have one on the ship.

He shivered, echoes of that swift vision bringing him goose-bumps. Did she know about his occasional slip with Okalani? To shake the feeling, he approached the table, hoping to call the meeting to order.

The gathered captains, however, were not ready to settle down. Spirited conversations continued in the corners, and liquor from the sideboard poured liberally into glasses and thick mugs. Each ship had provided a tray of delectable items to feed those in attendance, which left a wide range of choices. With a loud, growling rumble, Temms' stomach protested the fact he had skipped a morning meal to make his final plans.

He surrendered to the inevitable and helped himself to a plate of cold cuts and thin-sliced brown bread, layering on two different spicy spreads to complement the meats. He took a seat midway down the side of the main table, and let someone bring him a bright-labeled bottle from the local brewery and a tall glass.

Wanting to be finished eating before the meeting began in earnest, so his mouth and mind were focused on the business at hand, he chewed his food, savoring the fresh tastes, and washed it down with the nutty ale. He knew more than half those in attendance, and had heard of several of the others, cataloguing them by reputation.

C. T. Dutton had the background most similar to Temms himself, retired from the Presidium, a planetary security and expeditionary force based on Terza, the third planet in the system. Though he had never married, it was said he and Kyndra had met soon after he became a mercenary, and he hadn't been able to leave her since. He had hinted at a child, but Temms had never laid eyes on her.

Several others, including Lin Hocai and Xi Pinsan, a young sister and brother who flew together, were locals who had grown up in the Agency mold. The pair dressed alike, as if they were twins, and preferring clothing in their families' tradition of light silk jackets and tight black pants. They had been nurtured and lauded for awhile as the bright young faces of the next generation of the Agency. They had become disaffected after a few years, however, and they had moved on.

Temms had always wondered how they were able to escape. One of these days, he would ask them. It might present a way inside.

The two had joined in lively conversation with Tommy and two young women, one dark-haired with brown eyes that snapped fire, and the other a curvy blonde. They were easily the most attractive women in the room.

That's my boy.

Chuckling at his burst of pride, he set his plate aside, and then pulled out his notes.

Tommy was right. The Agency was up to something.

After their late-night talk, Temms had called together what senior officers weren't bedridden and they had come up with some possibilities. He had heard, informally, from an officer on another ship, who had heard from someone on another vessel, that the sleek black Agency ships had been spotted in increasing patrols around Marriel and its moons. Could it be coincidence that was the same area in which Temms usually flew his ship?

Doubtful, and this is why. I've not been circumspect with my views on the Agency.

Using the same logic that had caused his former captain to christen Temms' ship with its unusual name, he knew the blame would fall square on him. When the ugly holos of Jak Moster's battering circulated among the mercenary ships, and the *Ramman's* new commander Ral avoided contact with them, that sealed the deal.

The Agency was stepping up its game. Something was coming. Not only should the captains get themselves prepared, but it would be behoove them to perhaps consider a first strike. With any luck, he might be just the person to lead that.

"All right!" he shouted over the babble of voices. "Let's get to this before the Agency decides to pay us a visit. Any of you swabs want to end up like Jak?"

That brought the room to dead silence.

Now that he had their attention, Temms continued. "Please, take your seats."

Across the room, Tommy peeled himself away from the blonde and came to stand behind his father, while the rest settled in. The blonde consoled herself by taking the arm of a broad-shouldered man dressed simply in a button-down shirt and blue work pants, wearing some kind of tooled leather boots and a leather vest. A broad-brimmed hat sat on thick hair the color of desert sand. Choosing a seat opposite Temms, he seated the blonde to his right and the dark-haired girl to his left with a proprietary air.

Had Tommy seen that? The boy might end up disappointed in that particular department. Poor kid.

He cleared his throat. "I'm Temms Rogers of the cargo ship *Doubtful*, for those of you who don't know. I called this meeting to address the problem of the Agency, and its effect on our rights to do business."

"So we know who's here, I'd like you all to introduce yourselves. We're not recording this and no one's taking names. Far as I'm concerned we're all just brothers, and this is one big family reunion."

A mild but nervous laugh made the rounds, and then Dutton introduced himself and Kyndra, as did the twins. The man in the hat took it off and stood to make his introductions. His speech was slow, his vowels drawled, and his grin both shy and genuine.

"I'm Garrett Rawls, come from a planet called Earth which ain't in your system here. Not sure how I got here, exactly, but somehow I got sucked through some kinda wormhole."

Temms' interest perked up. Another ship had arrived in this universe the same way he had? What kind of experiment were these ancient aliens playing?

"My ship got bunged up some, but it's straightened around now, thanks to these two." He gestured to the blonde and then to the brunette, a real looker with coffee-colored skin. "This here's Nikki, and this is Valeni Pascual. They've showed me around and been right hospitable."

"Our ship is the *Six-Shooter*," Val added.

Dutton leaned over to Temms "Don't let that pretty, fluffy outside fool you," he whispered. "Those girls are dangerous with a firearm."

Temms filed that information away. "Welcome, Mr. Rawls, and ladies."

The introductions continued. Tommy ducked away to stand near the door, engaged in a conversation with no one at all. Nim broke off conversation with a couple of captains Temms didn't know and came back to the vicinity of the table, his eyes on his captain. When everyone had a piled-high plate of food and a seat, Temms started with the most difficult news on his agenda.

"I'd hoped someone from the *Ramman* would be here. Last I'd heard no one had come up with Jak's body. Has anyone received an update?"

Curious looks were exchanged among the attendees, but no one spoke up.

"We've all seen the holo. We can hope he survived. I think it's fair to say that none of us are immune from similar treatment. Do we all agree on that?" He paused, expecting no one would answer.

He was right.

"They're getting serious. Which means they are taking us seriously, too, as a threat."

The door opened, admitting no one, and then closed.

"Think that means they're serious about someone," said a man seated across the table, eyeing Temms. "Sounds to me like they're worked up over the man who's been collecting the artifacts."

In the brief silence that followed, Tommy returned to his place, standing at parade rest behind his father. Nim moved to take up a position directly opposite, giving the impression the room was covered.

"So what are we gonna do?" asked a man seated across the table. "I say we just suck it up. It's not that bad. Just a constant hand out for money. Pretty much like every other petty government around this sector."

"Not that bad for me, either," said another captain Temms didn't know. "Just a quarterly reminder."

A general assent rippled around the table.

Temms' neck tensed, ready for an argument. "They're practically chasing my ship down and reading memos over my shoulder."

He glanced at C. T., who just shrugged. Was he receiving special scrutiny? Why would that be? "No one else is getting new demands? If it's me now, it could easily be one of you next quarter."

"What choice do we have?" the first man asked. "We're outmanned, outgunned. None of the councils are willing to help us."

"True. Though I can't see why."

Dutton broke in. "If we were somewhere like the Kalindan system where the government regulates everything we might be able to deal directly with a council. As it is, too many of the governing units on Marriel and Terza are small, and they don't control enough territory to exert a lot of authority. The Agency comes in with a piddly kickback, and the councils are happy not to have to mount a patrol force of their own."

Temms persisted. "You'd think it would be to their advantage to get rid of the Agency's interference. Hells, they could collect the tax themselves. Surely regional coffers could benefit if they got their cut straight from us."

"Don't see why we should have to pay anything to anyone," Lestand growled. "Not like they cover our fuel or flights."

"Exactly my thinking, Lestand. Hasn't anyone tried to buck the Agency?" Temms asked. "A concerted effort to run them off or at least negotiate a fairer deal?"

"Not anyone still alive," Dutton said.

That sober thought stalled discussion for a few minutes. People ate their food and didn't look each other in the eye. That couldn't be where it would stop. He wouldn't let it.

"I'm open to ideas. Anyone have some?"

"Coupla seasons ago," Xi Pinsan offered. "Jak tried to organize a blockade, with a dozen or so ships keeping mercenaries from taking the cargoes to our regular ports. But there's too much space out here to stop every one. They just find some way around it. The persistent ones will get through. Then the whole exercise is pointless."

"What about a hostile takeover?" Rawls interjected.

"A what?" Puzzlement manifested around the table.

"When my daddy wanted to shut down a competitor, he'd launch a takeover."

Lestand scoffed. "How can you take over something when you're not wanted?"

"You don't let'em know it's you. Hornswoggle 'em a bit." As confused looks came his way, he leaned in and put his elbows on the table. "In order to own a company and make decisions, you got to own a majority of it. Then you're in control. Daddy had enough cash sitting around he could get his buddies to buy up bits of the stock, the ownership rights of the company, so that all told, he'd own a majority. Then he could walk into the stockholders' meeting and tell them how things was gonna run."

A roar of conversation popped up around the table, some of it derisive, others thoughtful. Temms let it play for a few minutes, wanting the thought to sink in his own mind for consideration. He had certainly heard of such shenanigans back on Gilada from other officers who played the financial markets, but he had never understood such things. He would rather look someone in the eye if they had a conflict, and face them down till it was over.

Although that way you more often tended to end up dead.

He knocked on the table for attention. "Anyone else have something to contribute? I'm sure we haven't heard all the ideas yet. Don't be shy."

That opened the floor to a flood of protests, a few shouting loud enough to be heard over the rest.

"It's not like the Agency has a way we can buy in!"

"A total waste of time trying." That man, dark-skinned, his head shaved bald, shoved his chair back from the table. "A real waste of time. I thought you had a solid plan to keep our ships safe and our pockets full. All this is gonna do is get us all killed. Just like Jak."

He beckoned to the officer who had accompanied him, and they walked for the door. It opened as they approached and closed behind them as they left, without their touching it.

A buzz of unrest followed, during which Temms tried to refocus the discussion. "Could we get people on the inside then? Someone who had be a voice of reason?"

Lestand laughed. "You see any volunteers here?" He waved his hand to include the others at the table. "Anyone want to waltz on in to the Agency ranks as a spy?"

No hands went into the air, but Temms really hadn't expected to see any.

"I feel certain they'll try to get someone in ours." He studied them all with his steely gaze. "But none of you are spies. I'm confident of this."

Nikki eyed him. "And how can you be so sure?"

Temms snapped his fingers.

A hushed horror swept over the group as two reptilians taller than even the tallest man there materialized by the door. They stood upright, uniformed, their scaly brown faces and golden eyes surveying those in the room. Heavy boots covered their feet, but at the ends of their fingers, two inch long deadly claws protruded, awaiting Rogers' command.

He knew they could appear in human form as well, olive-toned skin and black hair suggesting an ethnic heritage from the other side of Marriel, but Aronka and her mate Tabio were Bellonans, shape-shifters whose natural capabilities included cloaking themselves from light, essentially rendering themselves invisible. He had wanted them in this form today, just to make his point. They were perfect security officers. Discreet and deadly.

Temms stood. "I am fortunate to have a Bellonan security team, and I assure you they have checked out everyone here. Anyone who did not pass scrutiny would not have entered. Or left."

Kyndra faced the reptiles a moment, closing her eyes as she took their empathic measure, and then she turned back to Rogers with a nod.

"We comprise a unique and diverse group," Temms went on. "Each of us has at least one officer aboard with a special skill, something the Agency will perhaps not anticipate. What other alliances might we expect to make other than ourselves?"

Valeni leaned forward, her low cut blouse attracting the attention her soft voice might not have carried. "Right now the average person buying goods doesn't realize or doesn't care that the Agency is gouging us. Maybe we should find a way to let them know exactly what the Agency's doing. The councils—"

"You can't depend on the governmental councils, girly," interjected one gray-haired pirate from across the table. "Buncha old-boy-network sheep."

Valeni's eyes flashed, and she was half out of her chair, knife in hand, when Rawls' blonde companion Nikki pulled her back into her seat. "Rumor has it the Agency isn't only concerned with the latest tariffs. A lot of questions are being asked about the Ancients' artifacts. Particularly some sort of space station they supposedly left behind, waiting to be discovered. Has anyone heard about this?"

Temms' ears perked up at the mention of the Ancients. A construction of those relics created the wormhole that had brought the *Doubtful* to these skies. A different composition of them had opened another long enough to send Jal Burko and his ship back to the other side, just in time to save Temms' crew.

But to date he had only found bits and pieces, building blocks, not a whole station.

Was this related to the odd midnight visit he had days earlier? Perhaps the station was the place the disembodied voice had referred to as a 'physical plant'. The Ancients asked for his help. It certainly behooved him to find it. Then.

"If anything's a rumor, it's that bleeding station," Lestand snapped. "Ain't no such thing and no use talking about it." He crossed his arms, a thundercloud gathered on his face.

"Where's it supposed to be?" Temms asked. "We've been from Marriel to Lennor and back and never came across anything like that. It's not inside the security systems on Perpetra, is it?"

The Prince and his brethren in the Consortium would no doubt be close-lipped about anything in their highly-guarded space. Their lives and livelihoods were based on high-tech solutions and superior weaponry. The Ancients' workings seemed to use more magic than technology. The engineers on the *Doubtful* only succeeded in creating the device to save the ship from Burko because that strange child Monty had an instinctive way with the pieces and parts.

Couldn't be them then. But where could such a construct exist?

"More importantly," Kyndra interjected, "the Agency is willing to pay for that kind of information."

"Like as not, they'll just beat it out of someone rather than pay," someone tossed in.

"Another reason not to get involved with this little conspiracy," said a dark-haired woman Temms hadn't met. Her body moved with nervous, jerky timing, head tilted slightly, her black eyes like a sparrow's.

"They're businessmen. There's always a cost of doing business," Temms said. His mind spun ahead, wondering what he might find aboard such a station. Their encounter with the Ancients when the machine Monty and Benzi Quinn had activated had touched them all. Was it possible they had left further enticements and instructions in this star's system? If the Ancients had set up a station as some sort of tutoring device for their offspring to find when they reached a certain level of advancement, then the fact they believed Rogers ready for the challenge was humbling.

The kind of power the artifacts could generate, though, was also humbling. The hand that wielded that power had to be the right one. Plenty of wrong ones could be on the lookout for it. What could the

Agency do with something like that? They had become even more of a terror to local merchant captains.

We can't let that happen.

"Please, people. This is clearly important. Perhaps if they're busy looking for this, we should be looking for it, too. Better we beat them to it."

"And what if those that follow you end up like old Jak?" said one of those who had spoken earlier. "Seems to me you've got a black mark on you that's a big old target to the Agents."

"So, someone else step up and take the lead, if you think I'm such a liability. I've got no ego involved in being leader of this."

Temms waited for someone to volunteer.

"That's what I thought. I've heard enough of you complain over the last year about the Agency and the tariffs and the way you're all treated. But no one's done anything. I'm ready to take them on."

He studied those seated at the table. "Is that it? You're all going to sit around and cry in your whiskey, then fold up and give whatever the Agency demands? Or do you want to do something about it?"

He got up from the table and visited the bar, getting himself another ale, letting the momentum ferment among those in the group. He had pegged the ones who weren't behind him, either verbally or by facial expression. Challenging the Agency was a radical notion. He couldn't expect to sell everyone just with a fresh face and a definite "maybe."

And what about this station, base, physical plant, whatever it might be? Did some of them know the location already? Perhaps they had their reasons not to share. He didn't intend to push them. Not yet. The time would come when the Agency would galvanize them all into action. He could wait.

All of us have our secrets, now, don't we?

He returned to the table, gradually feeling the energy in the room changing to his direction. "Pinsan, let's start with you. Tell us about the workings of the Agency and what you think are its likely vulnerable points."

When Pinsan started talking, warming quickly to his subject, Temms dismissed the Bellonans to wait outside so they wouldn't be a distraction. It wasn't long before every face at the table was lit with the excitement of real possibilities. They called out questions almost faster than they could be answered.

C. T. nudged Temms' elbow. "Looks like this might really turn into something useful."

Temms grinned. "As Liang always says, food must be eaten bite by bite, a road must be walked step by step."

Pinsan finished, his face flushed and triumphant as Hocai congratulated him on his presentation. "Thank you, Captain," he said.

"No, thank *you*, Pinsan. I think it's time we refreshed our cups and get serious about the discussion. Get another round, my friends, and let's wax creative!"

CHAPTER 6

COVERING engineering short-staffed had been a trial, but Benzi had managed, with a minimum of curse words.

He watched the operations of the heart of the *Doubtful* from the upper level deck where Dani Jamar's desk sat. She had this overview every day.

Like some buggin' queen, ruling over the peons below.

Though the pain of jealousy had faded over the months, it still burned Benzi. Rogers had lured him onto this ship by promising him the position of engineering chief, knowing full well he already had the head of the department solidly in place.

Well, he was up here now. Dani was flat on her back in the infirmary. If only it would last.

Below, five members of the engineering staff managed the daily assigned tasks that kept this ship in the air, monitoring the multiple consoles staggered around the main level and making trips to the lower deck to tend to the engines themselves. Benzi's office was off to the right, the only space in the room with a door to keep out the noise. The main entry to the workspace was directly across from where Benzi stood. Under the loft-style upper deck was an extended work area with large tables and other spaces to rebuild parts and stash projects.

Everyone looked busy and fulfilled. Benzi was in full control. Even his old, drunk, dead Da would have to admit he had come a long way.

And I ain't done making my mark on this universe yet.

Benzi's eye fell on the most senior engineer, a large, ugly biped from the planet Bricaster, covered in light gray fur like a rodent with a face malformed like a warthog. His name was Halian. Today he seemed slower and more difficult than usual. Most of the aliens Benzi had known thought they could get away with doing less than a man. Sure, Halian had been apologetic, but he had been underfoot all shift.

Wasn't like him really, but Benzi had been short on sleep and patience, too. Didn't matter if the old hulk had been around back in the days when Rogers first took this command, Halian had come just short of being booted out for the day.

Monty had actually been helpful, reconstructing a broken strut. His innate understanding of how things worked guided him to success. But he was plenty ready to leave the deck when Benzi finally closed his office door, running about thirty minutes past the scheduled end of his watch.

"Guess you've just got that something special, kid. Too bad you can't use that same ability to figure out regular communication, huh?"

Monty looked up at him with his usual confused stare.

"S'okay, snapper. You did good today." He ruffled the boy's hair and gave him one of Dani's butterscotch candies. Monty chortled with glee and ran ahead out of the office.

"Least I can make him happy. More than my old man did for me." Benzi sighed and headed in the direction Monty had gone. "Where are you, boy?"

Two hallways up from the door to engineering, Benzi lost visual contact with the boy, but suddenly heard his distressed keening. Tracking the sound, he turned a corner to find the boy kneeling next to a fallen Halian on the gray carpet, tears streaming down his face. He shook the large hunk of alien, lying unresponsive on his back and completely blocking the hallway.

"Sick, Pop, sick."

What was he, some kind of veterinarian? The oversized engineer had been upright just minutes before. What could have smacked him down so quick?

"Sprechan's balls. Hal? Hal!" He leaned over and shook the massive shoulder, but Halian didn't even twitch. His eyes remained closed and his skin turned even grayer than usual.

"Sick," Monty said.

"Yeah, boy, I get it. He's sick all right."

"Sick," the boy whispered.

"Right." Doing his best not to snap at the kid's perseverating, Benzi took him by the shoulders and stood him up, hunkering down to look him right in the eye.

"Look here, you. I want you to run along quick to Dr. Okalani and tell her to send a transport up here. She can get him hauled down there and then—" He shrugged, not sure what kind of prognosis might be forthcoming.

Monty's eyes slowly widened. "Die?"

The anguish in that single word stabbed Benzi to the core. He had to get the kid's mind focused in a more positive direction.

"No, Snapper. Hal? Hellsafire, he'll be here after we're long gone. The doc'll get him fixed up just fine, you'll see. Now run!"

The boy straightened and took off in the direction of the infirmary.

The thrum of the engines rumbled like distant thunder in the empty hallway. Benzi eyed Halian. The big alien's breath wrestled with his chest in an effort to escape, and then fought to re-enter. Was it the lying on his back part that was wrong? Silently berating himself for allowing pity for a wog, Benzi crouched down and heaved his shoulder against Halian's, trying to roll him over onto his side.

The effort jarred Benzi's teeth together, and he tasted blood when he bit his tongue.

"Sprechan's ass, man," he lisped through the pain. "What are you doing? Don't break yourself on account of no wog." He curled away from Halian, gingerly holding his tongue in the center of his mouth. "Let the doc handle it. S'what she gets paid for, unless you count the fringes she gets from the Cap."

Benzi's mother had left him and his Da for an ugly, crusty alien. He had never trusted wogs since. He didn't owe them a damned thing. He stared at the wall, trying to ignore the graying skin and labored breathing of the alien. Then that despised pity crept in again, and he relented. "Damn me, I can't leave him like this."

This time, he put his back to the wall and planted his feet square against Halian's thick arm. Digging his toes under Halian's shoulder, he slowly straightened his knees, pushing with all his might until the big alien flopped over on his side. The pressure released, Benzi crashed to the floor ass first, sending a wave of pain up his spine.

His groan echoed down the hall, and he fell sideways, holding his aching noggin. When he opened his eyes, he found himself staring at Halian's wide hind end. His stunned, tingling nerves wouldn't even let him move away. He was stuck.

Didn't stop him from trying, though. He rocked a little toward the wall, but his arm went numb.

"Bleeding fried chicken gums!" he growled through clenched teeth.

Footsteps hurried down the corridor on the far side of his feet.

"Pop?"

"Sweet heavens," Okalani said with a gasp. "Both of them? Lavan, you check Benzi."

The doctor came into Benzi's view, tendrils of her blonde hair flying loose from a band she had tied around her head. Medi-scanner in hand, she listened to Halian's chest, her eyes closed.

Lavan's broad body blocked his view, and he protested, biting his tongue again.

"Damn it!

"Whoa. Quinn?" Lavan pulled back, eyeing Benzi. "Thought you were out cold."

"Just wish I was," he muttered. "Help me up."

The burly orderly easily hoisted Benzi to his feet, setting him down more gently than Benzi expected. Then Monty threw himself at the wounded engineer, grabbing on tight.

"Ow! Snapper, please!" Benzi sagged at the knees.

Okalani spared him a glance. "What happened?"

"Hal couldn't breathe, so I shoved him over. Bleeding bastard weighs about a ton. Thought I'd bust a gut muscle."

"How long has he been like this?"

Benzi shrugged, and then regretted it, as an ache grabbed his shoulder muscles and clamped down hard. "Finished his watch upright. But he'd definitely not been himself all day."

"Lavan, prop him up and get the hovercart. Halian's heart is in arrhythmia. He needs to be in the infirmary. Now."

"Yes, ma'am."

Lavan stepped around Benzi, who leaned against the wall. Monty still clamped hard to his legs, and brought the flat board to lay next to the unconscious Bricasterian on the floor. He and Okalani pulled and shoved till the big alien lay on the cart. Okalani activated the hover part of the craft, and it rose with a large creak into the air, just short of waist height. The doctor and orderly each took a side.

"Benzi, come along. I want to get you checked out. You're bleeding and you don't look good."

He grunted in protest. "Ah, come on, Doc. Ain't I had enough for one day?"

"No argument, pal. You come along now or I'll call Liang."

His eyes narrowed. *Like I'd let that cold fish see me at my worst.* "Fine, fine, then. Have it your way."

But she was already halfway down the corridor, guiding the cart toward the lift.

Aching in every joint, he followed, Monty half-supporting, half-clinging to him.

When they arrived at the infirmary, Okalani gestured Benzi into a chair by the door. She and Lavan unloaded Halian onto the last available exam bed. Riviera and Dani occupied the two others. Neither of them were awake. Riviera had some kind of breathing apparatus attached.

The impact of what he saw sank into him slowly, bringing a cold chill right into his bruised bones. He had thought Dani was down with a stomach bug or something, but this looked serious. Okalani's grim expression while she tested the now-gasping Halian with several different pieces of equipment did nothing to dispel Benzi's growing alarm.

"Hey, Doc, I'm not gonna catch what they got, right? Not by just sitting here?"

Belatedly, he remembered Monty sitting by his side. "Not the boy, neither?"

No answer. Something started beeping.

"Life support!" Okalani barked. "Hurry!"

Lavan disappeared into the back room, and then returned, balancing several pieces of apparatus, which he hooked up to the bed. Okalani scrambled for a cabinet full of clear bottles and filled several syringes from them, injecting into the alien, who hadn't moved once since they had brought him. His breathing rattled deep into his thick chest, each breath coming harder and harder.

"Doc?"

Monty whimpered beside him, and Benzi's arm instinctively slipped around the boy. This couldn't be happening. This couldn't—

The beeping turned into a solid, mournful tone.

Okalani went into frantic action, thumping Halian's chest. "No! Hal!"

Lavan, too, tried his magic with the equipment he had brought, but nothing revived the alien. A weeping Okalani laid a white sheet over him. Halian was dead.

Benzi's heart raced. He and Monty had been with Halian all day, working side by side. He had touched Hal in the corridor. They both had. Were they going to be next?

His bruised muscles protesting, he twisted around to examine the boy. His eyes certainly seemed bright, and he didn't appear to have trouble breathing. "How do you feel, snap?"

The boy hunched down into his chair, his moist eyes welling over with tears. "Sad."

"Right, but do you hurt?" He felt the boy's forehead, but it remained cool, not fevered. An ear to Monty's chest revealed no difficulty breathing.

He took several deep breaths, and found no signs in himself either.

Well, what in Sprechan's name?

Lavan finally remembered they were waiting. "Doctor, shall I check Quinn?"

Okalani rubbed her hands across her damp face. "Yes. Yes, they should be examined. I—I'll have to call Temms." She walked into her office and shut the door.

Lavan bowed his head a moment, and then picked up his medi-scanner, bringing it over to read both Benzi and Monty. After he'd gone through one time, he did it a second.

"What's the matter?" Benzi demanded. "What did you find?"

Lavan shook his head, a puzzled expression on his face. "Nothing. You're perfectly healthy."

"Monty, too?"

The orderly nodded. "Not a sign."

Benzi's engineer's mind was still rushing ahead, putting clues together. "But hold on. First Dani. Then Hal." He tried to remember whether Riviera had been in engineering in the last several days. She and Dani had been collaborating on some project in hydroponics. Had they met in his space?

He recalled at least one time, maybe two, that were recent, but he couldn't remember if it had been just before Dani had called off.

"Maybe it's something in engineering." He explained his thought process. "Not that we've got anything new there. All the equipment's been installed for months, and we ain't even had new lubricants, as far as I remember. But if they've all been there, we'd better evacuate the place, right quick."

Okalani emerged from her office, her face pale, her eyes puffy and sad. "The captain's coming down."

"Quinn's got a theory, ma'am." Lavan straightened up and shared Benzi's thought process.

"Riviera was there, too?"

Benzi nodded. "Several times in the last couple weeks."

"Who's down there now?"

Benzi cocked his head, recalling who had come on duty at end of watch, and he counted them off, ticking on his fingers. "Iov, Uri, Zandra Cilka and Fayler." A troubled twitch ran through his stomach. "But we ain't got remote controls, Doc. Can't run the boards from anywhere else in the ship. Someone's got to stay there. Else the ship don't run."

The captain walked in the door. "What's this about the ship not running?"

His gaze scanned the room, falling last upon the sheet-covered hulk of Halian's body. "The ship has to run. I don't know how many more losses we can stand."

CHAPTER 7

TEMMS had hardly been able to understand Okalani's words, so choked they were with tears, but he caught the gist.

Struggling with denial, he was out of his chair before he had even made his reply. His heavy footsteps echoed along the corridors that connected his office to the medical suite, heavy like his heart. Halian had been with him every day of this command. Losing him was like losing a part of the ship. Or his own soul.

Gripping the throat of his cascading emotion, he sublimated it long enough to walk in to medical like he was under control. Quinn's words knocked him loose.

"What in hells are you talking about? What's wrong with the ship?"

Okalani took his arm, but he shook her off.

Quinn's eyes narrowed and he got to his feet, facing Temms square on. "Ain't said nothing's wrong with the ship, Cap. But we got three down what's been working there and I surely don't intend to be the next one."

Okalani wiped her eyes and shoved her hands in the pockets of her lab coat. "I still don't have a handle on the origin of this illness, Temms. Mr. Quinn's theory is as good as anything I've got. Maybe there's a contaminant in engineering."

That was all he needed. Contamination on a closed vessel in space could be catastrophic. The longer he stood in the mid-sized room, the sharp smell of caustic cleaning fluids sank into his nose, with a strong undercurrent of unwashed bodies. Approaching the body of his dead friend and comrade-in-arms, Temms gestured at the other two beds. "How are they?"

The doctor shrugged. "No improvement. Riviera's holding her own with a heavy amount of breathing support. I'm hoping Dani's unconscious state is giving her body time to heal. They haven't gotten worse in the last two shift-turns. I've got to hold on to hope for them."

"They have the same thing that took Hal?"

Just saying the words twisted the knife inside him.

Gone. Hal was gone.

"I don't know," she said. "I'll have to run some lab tests. Maybe with a large enough cross-section, I can find a common culprit." She turned to Lavan, who was checking Dani's IV line and smoothing her hair. "Let's get on that. Basic antibody testing, foreign substances, allergic reactions, anything that they each have. Especially if they've got it in common with Hal, at this point."

"Yes, Doctor." The man crossed to the supply cabinet to gather a tray full of instruments and syringes.

"I know this is heartbreaking for you, Temms," she said softly, reaching out to him.

He might have needed the comfort, but he couldn't let her inside his pain, not now. Setting his face like plascrete, he avoided her touch and pulled away. Instead, he turned his attention to Quinn, and Monty half hiding behind him. Both of them were rumpled and worn, but looked awake and healthy.

"What are you doing here? You're not coming down with this, too?"

"Sprechan's ass, I'd best not! Won't be a soul left." Quinn flexed his shoulders. "Monty here found Halian, and the wog half crushed me whilst trying to save him." He shrugged.

Rage flared through Temms at the casual dismissal of his long-time comrade as a *wog*. He grabbed the front of Quinn's shirt and shoved him up against the wall. "You'll speak of the dead with more respect, or I'll have you sent out an airlock."

Quinn sputtered and squirmed. "But I didn't mean nothing by it, Cap. Just that—you know."

"I know. I also know that I've lost my closest friend. No one needs your twisted worldview to cheapen his passing."

His heart whispered that he was overreacting. "Sorry, Quinn."

He released the engineer, who made a fuss of straightening his shirt and backing away. Something changed in the man's eyes.

"Sorry, Cap. Halian was a good engineer. He'll be missed."

A sigh escaped Temms. "All right. Get a team together to scour up engineering."

Quinn started to wind up again, and took a big breath to protest, but Temms cut him off.

"I know you're short-staffed. You can grab half a dozen of the new recruits from Sol Aeris. Decontam everything that might carry whatever this is. Pack up all the air filters, seal them tight. We'll dispose of them next stop."

"Yes, Cap. Right on it. Soon as the doc checks out Monty, here."

Dismissing Quinn, Temms returned to stand at Hal's bedside. He pulled the sheet down to have a last look. A series of scenes flashed through his mind, times spent drinking with the burly Bricasterian, late night card games, arguments, alliances. Hal never said much, but his strong determination had pulled Temms through many tough times.

"I can't believe he's gone," Temms said. So fast. That in itself was frightening. Could he lose the rest of his staff so quickly?

If the contaminant still existed in this hulk that once was a jovial companion, he would have to be removed from the ship as soon as possible. Temms couldn't remember Hal's exact wishes for post-death treatment, though he recalled they had discussed such things when they formed the plan to rebel against Burko's Confederation. Surely he had written it down somewhere.

He glanced again at Halian's body, and steeled himself. "We'll find a place to bury him. Somewhere natural. With trees."

Annoyed with himself for failing to protect his friend and angry at the situation in general, Temms turned back to the room, finding Quinn still standing there. "Didn't I give you an order? Get on it, Quinn!"

Monty stiffened, his eyes wide with fear.

"This stops here," Temms growled at Okalani. "We can't afford to lose anyone else."

"Understood, sir." She chewed her bottom lip and looked away. She probably needed a hug. Hells, they all did. This just wasn't the time.

What had he been doing before this sidetracked him? Oh, yes. He had been on his way to meet with one of the damned Agents, who had requested "just a few moments" of his time.

Well, he would give him some time. And he would let all this frustration loose, too. That Agent might be very sorry he had even asked for a meeting.

* * *

OVERWHELMED, Okalani stood in the center of her infirmary and collected herself.

The familiar sounds of Lavan's puttering at Dani's side gradually fell into place. Monty whimpered and pulled at Quinn's sleeve. The awareness released her. She took back her role. Here, in this room, she was a doctor in charge of her patients. When Temms was around, the last thing she felt was that she was in control.

"Mr. Quinn, what else can I do for you?" she asked.

His sapphire eyes lit up for a moment, and she wondered if he was thinking about propositioning her, for what might be the tenth time. Or the fiftieth. His mouth opened, but after he looked in her eyes nothing came out.

It wasn't that Benzi Quinn wasn't a handsome man. He was. He knew it, too. That smile had likely broken many hearts over the years. But Okalani's heart had already latched onto one man, whether he wanted it or not. It was protected against random intruders.

"Pop sick?" Monty asked, in a very small voice.

"Let me check that again," Okalani said, and she came to the engineer, checking his back, the lump on the side of his head. "That's going to be sore for a few days. I can give you something for pain—"

"Eh. Got something that'll do." He pulled away from her, gaze downcast. "Thanks, Doc. I'll take care of it. C'mon, snap. We got work to do."

He swept the boy up in his arms and stalked out.

That left Okalani with only her duties before her. She had been stung by Temms' dismissal of her, but Quinn had been there. They had always shared a tacit agreement to keep their loose liaison quiet, so perhaps he had just reminded her, a little less subtly than was kind. But afterward, he wouldn't even look her in the eye. Was it more than a wish for discretion? Or had this blow hit him that hard?

Either way, didn't hurt any less.

With Quinn ordered to proceed with a decontamination sweep of engineering, that left her to form the next potential theory. If Quinn found something, so much the better. If he didn't, she had better be ready to try another tactic.

The addition of Halian to the list of affected patients triggered her into a path of investigation that had only buzzed on the edges of her conscience before that. She plopped into her desk's chair and tapped in a request to access Dr. Montgomery's files from before the crossover through the wormhole. The only ones to come down with this mystery illness were those who came with the captain from the other universe. Logic dictated that it was some virus or bacteria that they had brought with them.

And the fact that Hal had sickened and died within a work shift, while the two women had a more lingering and slow decline, that would be significant in the differential diagnosis process.

She entered a listing of tests she wanted to perform on the dead Bricasterian's remains before he was moved into cold storage pending burial, and sent it to Lavan's personal monitor for the gathering of samples. Whatever had struck him down had moved so quickly, it should be rampant in his system. Once she could determine what had done this, she would be better able to protect the rest of the crew.

Sure the crew had all heard of Halian's death, she composed a brief memo to remind the crew that all anti-infectious protocol precautions should be in place. She sent the memo ship-wide, and then checked on Riviera and Dani. No improvement on either of them. Rather, their life signs were sliding into the range of poor prognosis. Both remained unconscious. She had to hope this meant that their body's own defense systems were absorbing all the resources the body had to fight the infection.

If that's what it was.

She had know before long. One more round of tests across the three patients should give her a wide enough cross-section of data to hazard a good guess. It better be a good one. If she couldn't get a line on this, she had no way to protect the other members of this crew from the fate that had taken Halian.

She couldn't fail them. Or Temms Rogers.

CHAPTER 8

TEMMS waited by the rear hatch on the second deck, where the Agency ship *Shelim* was scheduled to dock any moment. The room had little to distinguish it, gray metal walls, large empty floors, entrance to an air lock. Without anything to distract him, Temms could only brood about what might happen in the next few hours.

When the *Doubtful* had been hailed by the *Shelim* almost as soon as they had left Marriel orbit, his heart had shuddered, apprehension temporarily displacing the pain of losing his friend.

Were they really watching him so closely that they had known about the meeting? The captains had agreed to keep each other notified of any suspicious Agency activity, but to his knowledge, no one else had reported trouble or contact from the enemy.

Maybe I'm the first.

The captain of the *Shelim*, Agent Delcin, had suggested a meeting on the surface, but Temms had summarily rejected that option. Too easy to get ambushed on the planet. He would have preferred not to meet at all, but avoiding the confrontation would likely incite the Agency to more aggressive tactics.

The one thing he could say about the Agency is that they didn't surrender easily.

Therefore, his best bet was to control as many of the circumstances as possible. He hadn't known what reaction he would get to his invitation. But he should have expected the Agent would have been cocky enough to take the challenge of meeting on Temms' ground.

Tommy tapped an annoyed toe behind him.

"You know this is one of the more stupid things I've seen you do?"

His son's tone rubbed a raw nerve. "If you can't handle the security detail, Chief," Temms snapped.

Tommy's jaw fell. "Sorry. It was—" He looked around at the empty room. "Just us."

Temms stepped close and dropped his voice. "Attitude matters. As you so strongly pointed out, we're running a big risk letting these people so close. Can they scan inside our ship? I'm not sure. Is what we want them to hear just before they come over that we're divided? We can't afford to be vulnerable for one moment."

The young man's gaze dropped, though his shoulders stood just as high. "Of course. I'm sorry."

Satisfied his point had hit home, the captain squeezed Tommy's arm, the feel of the old Confederation uniform odd under his fingers. He had instructed Tommy to dress in formal uniform. Temms had tried one on, but the stretchy fabric had pulled at Temms' neck, reminding him of the noose the Confederation had become to him at the end.

No, thank you.

He chose instead a particularly bright blue tropical shirt with birds all over it. If he was going out, it would be in his own style.

Waiting for the door to open, he straightened his shoulders and looked at the ceiling, speaking quietly. "We've got to keep control of this situation, even though we've got trouble on all sides. Okalani's going to get my people back on their feet, and we're going to take our right place in this universe, without the Agency sniffing up our butts all the time. It's going to happen, right?"

"Yes, sir."

Tommy met his eyes, full of courage and determination. They were back on the same page.

The door to the interior corridor opened, admitting Aronka, tall even in her human form and serious-faced, her golden eyes cold and without feeling. Her midsection was rounded gently, reminding Temms of her pregnancy.

"Captain," Aronka said, with a nod of greeting.

"Taking the day off?" he asked.

"Tabio wished to spend the day with Rey. Engineering reported a nest of voles on the lower deck, and he intended to teach him to hunt." She smiled, her teeth perfect and straight. "It will not be long until my confinement, so I desired the chance to be on duty."

Temms didn't know much about the Bellonans' birthing process, and he didn't want to. But he remembered from the birth of Rey the year before that Aronka and Tabio both locked themselves away for several weeks. After that, it took several more to air out the lower deck. The smell had been indescribable.

"The corridor's secured?" he asked, just above a whisper.

"Yes, Captain. We have sealed off all the doors that lead off this deck. If there is unanticipated trouble, the Agents will be contained."

"Very well."

He didn't know what sort of delegation the Agency would send, but he had purposely limited his team. Liang had requested the opportunity to attend the meeting, but he couldn't get the holo of Moster and his first officer out of his mind. In the event the encounter turned treacherous, he didn't want to put both himself and Liang at risk.

He had agreed to meet without weapons, so neither he nor Tommy were armed. Difficult to imagine anyone getting past Aronka, though. That reassured him.

Metal scraped on metal outside the hatch, and all three came to attention. Tommy posted himself on Temms' right. Aronka moved to their left and faded from view.

Tasiq's voice came over the intercom. "Captain, Agent Delcin is requesting permission to board."

"Understood. You've got the room jammed?"

"Yes, sir. No one will be able to scan anything else on the ship from inside."

"Well done." He cleared his throat. "Showtime," he muttered, still wishing he had a weapon on his hip.

When the Agents entered the lock, he scanned them, not finding any obvious weaponry, but that didn't mean they were home free. Rumor had it that the Agency obtained, by force or otherwise, all sorts of secretive new tech from the ships it encountered. They might have a new arsenal undetectable by the usual means. He just didn't know. He would have to take the gamble.

Once the lock controls showed the air pressure had equalized, Temms tapped the blue button to open the hatch. It clanked to the right, showing the door to the *Shelim* was pressure-sealed behind three men in the stiff black uniform of the Agency.

The man in front was tallest, his hair a steely gray, and the insignia on his collar twice as plentiful as the other two, who could have been dark-haired, dark-eyed twins, handsome and square-jawed. Their shoes shined as if power-polished, as did every silver button on the double-breasted jackets.

Brow furrowing in disapproval as he took in Temms' clothing, the gray-haired man cleared his throat. "I'm Agent Delcin. These are sub-agents Indro and Elden."

Temms let his gaze sweep over the three men, purposely waiting to invite them further in until Aronka could catch a whiff of any kind of bio-weapon they might have concealed. It also gave him a chance to push their patience buttons. The thought brought a slight smile to his face.

Hearing nothing from her, he finally stepped aside. "Agents, welcome to the *Doubtful*."

Stern-faced, they came aboard, their boots clanging against the metal floor of the bay. They stood near the hatch, arms stiff at their sides. Finally, Delcin sniffed audibly.

"Are you transporting animals aboard, Captain?" he asked.

Was it possible the Agents could detect the Bellonan? No one else had been able to do so. Temms kept his expression pleasant, and ignored the smarmy smile twitching at the Agent's lip. "Absolutely not. You and I both know we'd owe a special tax for that."

They glared at each other in silence for a moment. Then Tommy coughed. "Perhaps I could show you to the conference room that's been prepared for your meeting."

"Of course," Delcin said. "Let's get to business."

Temms nodded to Tommy, who turned away and marched out into the corridor. Temms held out his hand in invitation for the agents to follow the chief, and he followed behind them. Aronka must have come, too, moving silent as the wind.

The meeting room was a converted cargo bay on the ship's starboard side. Two broad ports in the wall revealed the burnished black silhouette of the *Shelim* outside. In the center of the room sat a rectangular table with a *faux* wood veneer surface, and eight chairs. Large crates stacked up against the far walls, their markings turned toward the wall.

Temms took the seat at the nearest end of the table, offering Delcin his choice of the other chairs. He took the one on Temms' immediate right. The proximity of the grim-faced man gave him the willies, but he stiffened his resolve. Tommy stood, on alert, just behind his captain, in easy reach of Delcin. The other agents sat to Delcin's right, the three forming a solid wall of perceived force.

A uniformed ensign entered the room with a cart of refreshments, including iced water and small trimmed sandwiches of meat and cheese, which she set in the center of the table. Delcin studied the food as if it was likely full of poison.

Temms grinned. "It's not often we get such esteemed visitors," he said. "We want to make sure you feel welcome."

He pushed the tray closer to Delcin and his men, but did not help himself to the food. No sense in reassuring them it was safe to eat. Certainly, it was. But it satisfied him to play this little mind game.

"You gentlemen asked for the meeting. Is there a particular agenda?"

Delcin's smile coalesced slowly, as though he consciously had to assemble it. "I hate to limit myself, Rogers. You never know exactly what

I'm going to find interesting."

"Suit yourself."

Temms' estimate of how long this session might take tripled. He set an electronic note pad in front of him. He had anticipated topics of conversation, including the rumored place of the Ancients. Better to distract the Agent as far from that one as possible. "Let's start with my formal protest to your most recent rate increase. What gives you the right to arbitrarily hike what we owe?"

Delcin didn't blink but Indro stiffened.

They didn't anticipate me leading with open rebellion. Good. Let's keep them guessing.

Delcin put a black hide-covered briefcase on the table and clicked it open.

Tommy moved behind Temms, angling closer so he could see the contents in the case.

The agent removed a single elongated electronic pad and set it in front of him, and then moved the case to the floor again. He activated the device, but the screen lay at an angle so Temms wouldn't be able to read it. After staring at if for several long seconds, he looked up and fixed Temms with a paternal gaze.

"I don't understand why you persist in believing we are enemies. As you know, the Agency serves the planetary councils, patrolling space around Marriel and Terza, and as much of Perpetran space, that which the Cartesian Consortium hasn't stolen for itself."

He paused, and Temms felt those hazel eyes analyzing him for a reaction. Temms' courtesies from the Consortium were no secret. Could they be a liability as far as the Agency was concerned?

Maybe that's what's got me on their radar.

When Temms didn't reply, Delcin went on. "Unfortunately, we serve at the whim of those councils. We're not in control of the rates they charge us to keep the spaceways safe for all who use them. Especially with more and more ships coming in from outside our system, our resources are strained to track them all." He read something on the screen, and then glanced at Tommy. "Get me a hot stimulant drink," he demanded in a patronizing tone.

Knowing Tommy's likely response, Temms held up his right hand to cut it off before it came out. "I'll send for something. Please be more specific."

A knowing look confirming the ploy, and its failure, Delcin just smiled. "Never mind. You've probably not got anything on board of the quality I'm used to." He sniffed and surveyed the room. "Considering these accommodations."

Were the Agents really this shallow? First, an attempt to get Temms alone, then insults to spark a fight? Ridiculous. It had to be some kind of test. "We wanted you to feel at home."

The Agent didn't miss a beat. "Clearly you've never been aboard one of our vessels. Due to our financial successes, we command a certain amount of luxury."

Temms glanced down the line to the other two Agents, whose eyes twinkled with amusement and approval. Did they want a test? He would give them one.

"Due to your spaceway piracy, you mean."

Delcin stiffened. "I expected you to be unreasonable, to rebel against any of our edicts. Jal Burko told us it was your way." His gaze captured Temms' and held it. "The way that got half your fleet killed."

The Agent's words hit Temms like a wave of icy water. Water that should have been long under the bridge. Sure, Burko, sucked through the wormhole on the *Doubtful*'s exhaust vapors, had allied himself with the Agency for his planned retribution against Temms. The rebellion he had started had damaged dozens of ships, preventing a dishonorable conquest of a planet.

But we didn't kill half the fleet.

His throat too tight to reply, Temms scrolled through some documents on his notepad, as if researching data. The longer he waited, the more satisfaction he felt from the Agents' side of the table.

Bastards. Burko, Delcin. Definitely two of a kind.

"I'm sure you're proud of your association with a snake like Burko. What was it he promised you exactly? His shiny new ship and all its technology?"

Eldin spoke for the first time. "No. He promised us yours."

The news didn't have its intended impact. Burko had confessed as much before his ship had been regressed to the far side of the wormhole once more. It didn't pain him any less.

"Ah. Well, you see the problem with that. It wasn't his to give." He eyed Delcin. "And it isn't for sale, either. Not for any amount of unjust tariffs."

"Well, you see the problem with that," Delcin said, echoing Temms' words and tone. "No one's really interested in your opinion."

Temms put the pad down with a loud click. "That's where you're wrong. It seems a number of people share my thoughts about your inequitable chokehold on the economy of this sector."

Delcin's smile was mild. "Would you care to provide their names? They can share the sanctions we intend to levy against you."

"No."

Temms shrugged. He could feel Tommy's annoyed tension radiating behind him, but the young man hadn't opened his mouth. A little maturity, and a hot pep talk, went a long way. So far, the conversation had progressed mostly as he thought it would. First the kid gloves, followed by a velvet-wrapped blade. How long would it be before that knife was unsheathed?

Delcin consulted his notes. "Your friends aren't as reluctant to speak of your seditious talk."

The statement concerned Temms. At this juncture he saw the game for what it was, a fishing expedition. They didn't really have anything, or they would confront him with it. He reached for one of the glasses of cold water and took a long drink. "I don't control what others say. Or what they do."

A smirk mirrored itself down the faces of the three Agents. Indro leaned forward until he had an unobstructed view of the captain.

"Captain, you underestimate your importance. We understand you're the ringleader of this threatened revolution."

Temms laughed. "Ringleader! Oh, my dear Agent, you must not understand how dire our situation is. I'm just one man, trying to run a business large enough to feed a crew. That's all. I'm not looking for trouble. I'm struggling from job to job, and I'm certainly not gifted with the amount of time I'd need to be some sort of modern Ket Willader."

The Agents stared at him blankly.

"Ket Willader? You've never heard of him? Back home, he was the best labor organizer in three star systems. Once he heard of an injustice being perpetrated, he'd hop on the next merchant ship and go handle it."

Tommy cleared his throat. "Perhaps Commander Burko failed to educate the Agents about our history on the other side."

"What? How could that be?" Temms stared at Delcin, expression carefully schooled in astonishment. "After all the information he shared with you, he didn't give you a data stick with all our history on it? How else can you possibly hope to uncover the mysteries of our existence?"

"It's hardly relevant," Delcin snapped. "You're no longer on his side of the wormhole. You're on ours. If you want to keep flying in our space, you *will* comply with our directives."

Temms eyed the Agent thoughtfully. "Space is pretty big. I think we have some other options."

"The new tariffs are due within the next cycle. You will pay in cash, technology or...."

As much as he wanted to resist, Temms' curiosity drove him to pick up that hook. "Or?"

Delcin leaned in. "We have intelligence regarding some sort of station on the edge of Perpetran space. The Consortium denies knowledge of such a construct. It may not belong to them. It may have been there in orbit before our current civilizations."

Temms' teeth chewed the inside of his lip. So it was true the Agency was after this station. What were the Ancients hiding there? "Well, knowing our circumstances as you do, you could understand why we wouldn't be likely to have knowledge of such a place."

"Perhaps not yet." The Agent again allowed his mouth to construct a smile, but no warmth lit his eyes. "Investigation has showed us your aptitude for finding what you need, even in foreign locations. Dealers who work with us report your search for artifacts that might have belonged to the Ancients. If anyone would be interested in this site and what it might provide, it would be Temms Rogers."

"And if I was?"

"Let's just say that information you could provide to us that leads to actual discovery might well offset any other financial obligation you'd have to pay tariffs. Depending on the extent of your personal involvement, of course. If you and your ragtag little bunch of rebels come in on the discovery together, I'm not sure we could extend the same sort of credit."

He tapped his screen and it went blank.

"Is it worth it to you, Captain?"

Doubtful, and this is why.

Temms didn't reply, his brain working at double speed to process the possibilities.

Delcin leaned closer. "It's a limited time offer, friend. Tuon Donn has set his attention on this acquisition. Do I need to say more?"

The name set off alarms. The seldom-seen head of the Agency had a reputation for getting what he wanted, regardless of the amount of bodies he left behind in his determination. Rumor had it he personally hired the mercenaries who carried out his dirtiest work, choosing only those whose cruelty was on a par with his own.

Bad news for everyone.

"Agent Delcin, I assure you I study all the alternatives before making decisions that impact my crew. This is something I'll have to consider, study, and discover if it's even possible."

Delcin nodded. "I like that you realize that your crew will share in any impact your decisions may have. Their well-being lies entirely within your control. Bad choices on your part could leave them vulnerable."

He hadn't raised his voice, but something dark underlined his tone. The threat brought the hackles up on the captain's neck. He pushed himself to his feet, his gaze slow to meet the Agent's, though when they finally locked eyes, he put the anger and resentment he felt into that look. "You don't know me. If you did, you'd know better than to make threats. It isn't the best way to appeal to my sense of duty."

Delcin and his men stood as well. "You didn't respond to the appeal to your duty. That would simply have involved a payment, as requested. You're the one who upped the stakes by refusing to pay. I'm simply calling your bluff."

"The non-aligned captains are struggling to stay in the air as it is. There's only so much blood you can get from a stone!"

"Perhaps." Delcin smiled again, the empty look of it sending a chill through Temms. "But crew members tend to have so much more."

Wanting nothing more than to wrap his fingers around the Agent's neck, Temms took a step back. The Agents were smart. They wouldn't begin a physical fight here. But they had surely drawn the line he had to cross. He couldn't let them provoke him.

Silence swallowed the next several long seconds. Finally, Tommy stepped toward the door. "If we're finished, allow me to show you out."

"I think we've made our point." Delcin pushed past Tommy, the others on his heels. Temms didn't follow. Better that he took the time to process a moment and get himself under control. He had heard other threats from them before, general ones, but Delcin's words had been directed right at Temms and his little family. Aronka likely accompanied the departing agents to the air lock, so Tommy would be safe.

Pulled in so many directions, Temms felt like he could explode. His people down sick with a mystery illness could leave his ship helpless. The Agency demanding raised tributes pushed the edges of what he could afford to pay—but if he didn't pay it, they could limit his ability to get jobs at all. Then where would he be?

And there was the plea of the Ancients, who had asked his help in finding some control device to activate the station, presumably before the Agency could appropriate it. Knowing he had those who remained healthy on his ship and others in the spacefaring community who might help was marginally comforting, but he knew the last word was his.

He walked to the port and watched the black ship pull away, wondering how much time he had before all he worked so hard to accomplish faced total ruin.

CHAPTER 9

WHILE others aboard openly grieved for Halian's loss, Liang suffered her heartbreak in silence. She found it difficult to sleep. Particularly when her dreams were haunted, not by the dead engineer, but by her old teacher, Rodolphus.

The dreams often took the same form. Roddi spoke to her from an amorphous cloud of shadows, urging her to find a specific object that had been lost or stolen. He never showed her exactly what it was, but he promised her great reward if she should locate it.

They disturbed her.

Every fiber of her being rejected the thought that Roddi would use material incentives as motivation. Roddi had never been interested in material goods. He had never taught that wealth or possessions were goals to be pursued, no matter how valuable. The important lesson he stressed for his students had always been individual moral development and improvement. This voice didn't ring true. The dichotomy always snapped her wide awake.

This night was no different.

Too distressed to return to sleep, Liang decided to put her energy toward something positive. She went to the computer and keyed in to study the medical data Okalani filed each day. Confidential though they might be, the medical reports were accessible through a special code Captain Rogers had given Liang a year before, for a very different purpose. Then, she had been altering records to show them as damaged, to keep loyalists from reading the truth about the *Doubtful's* arrival in this universe.

Now, she used the codes to gather as much information as she could about every detail on onboard life. It made her a better officer, and gave her quick intellect plenty of food for thought. When Rogers asked her for advice, she knew she could provide him the best possible intel, probably details even he hadn't ferreted out. It satisfied her need to be the best first officer she could be. She owed him so much. This, again, was small repayment for her rescue.

The reports, however, were troubling. Within seven days after the first reported case, science officer Riviera Brown and engineer Dani

Jamar remained in the infirmary. Halian's spirit had moved on.

She had read the reports describing the purge of the engineering section, and the precautions and remedies comported with her probable recommendations.

But then how did she explain the report on soft-spoken helmsman Kai Windthorp, who had gone to the infirmary earlier this morning complaining of intermittent difficulty breathing? The doctor had found the problem minor enough to collect samples for testing, and then release Kai to return to his quarters. No results posted yet.

And Tommy Rogers, too, had asked for something to help him sleep at night because his throat seemed to be seizing up.

Liang leaned back in her lightly padded chair and wrapped her fingers around her oversized mug, sipping the ginger-spiced tea within. The first three had connections to engineering, so a source of the illness seemed clear. But after the decontamination, that should have been the end of it.

Kai worked on the bridge.

Tommy worked in the security offices on the lowest deck.

Neither of them had much direct contact with engineering, although they might mingle with those crew members in other locations. So what was the connection?

The only one to die had been an alien. Halian was a large, muscular animal with humanoid features like a voice box and superior manual dexterity that allowed him to work magic on the engineering controls.

But they had other aliens on board. Tasiq, their communications officer, was a felinoid alien from Rogers' universe, whose auditory skills made him indispensable to the bridge crew. Tabio and Aronka were lizard-like shape-shifters, bred to provide security to royal families.

In the last year, the ship had also taken on three brothers, Muuvos who had transferred from a freighter coming from outside the system. She enjoyed engaging them in the ship's ongoing hand-to-hand combat competitions, because they were always good natured, even in a loss. Their short, stocky bodies were quite muscular. Copper-toned faces were anchored by large black eyes. Tiger-like stripes covered arms, legs, and matching extensive ridges on their ears. Their taste in clothing rivaled the captain's blinding tropical shirts, but left them not at all self-conscious. They had arrived with a crate of their planet's native instruments, which they played well, and taught others, too. Liang was particularly fond of their hand-carved flutes.

Five years separated the Muuvos, one from the other, the oldest, Iov, being nearly middle-aged in their culture, Nev, a young adult, and Uri in mid-adolescence.

But none of these other aliens showed the least bit of symptom.

Not restricted to males or females. Nor too old or too young. Not by department or hobbies.

The answer came to her so softly, that she nearly passed it by.

All of the afflicted were part of Rogers' original crew, Confederation officers. Perhaps some pathogen had come with them from that other universe.

Liang sat forward again and quickly reviewed Okalani's work. She saw nothing that confirmed this hypothesis, though she had logged a request for Dr. Montgomery's old records. She might be thinking along the same lines.

Liang loaded the information onto a handheld device and shoved her feet into her soft leather boots, and then headed for the infirmary. Perhaps she could be of help in the resolution of this killer mystery. The least she could do was try.

When she arrived, she found Dani and Riviera lying in the sickbeds, tubes running in and out of their bodies, looking like death itself. Lavan stood between the beds, a concerned look on his face and a spare oxygen canister in his hands. He turned, startled, at her entrance.

"You're not sick too, are you, ma'am?"

Liang shared a faint smile, intended to reassure him. "No. I wish to speak with the doctor. I might be of assistance."

He inclined his head toward the back of the medical suite. "She's taking some more samples. Or maybe an autopsy. She wasn't sure exactly what she needed."

He sighed and set the canister down, taking Dani's limp hand in his. "She's just got to recover from this. I swear she half-looks like an angel now."

Liang smiled gently at his intimate revelation of feelings for the sick woman. "I'll see the doctor, then."

She walked past him and into the back. Okalani was inside a brightly lit glassed-in room, a rack of test tubes and Petri dishes to her left, Halian's body on a table in front of her, covered from the waist down in a white sheet. The sight brought tears to Liang's eyes. Halian had always been kind to her, since the first day the captain had bought her freedom from that sleazy bar owner. She whispered a prayer for the peace of his soul and well-deserved rest on the far side of the sun.

After a respectful silence, she knocked softly on the glass.

Okalani glanced up. "I'll be out in a few minutes," she said. Her voice was muffled by the glass divider, but Liang nodded and stepped away. She had no need to watch the further surgical procedures. Instead she reviewed the notes she had made on Okalani's findings.

Okalani finally came out of the enclosure, turning off the lights, obscuring the body of their friend and colleague. Her shoulders hunched low and her eyes were puffy and red.

"You need some tea," Liang suggested. "Let me make you something to restore your energy."

Okalani's tired smile said it all. "Thank you so much." She sank into the chair behind her desk and dropped her head into her hands. "I haven't slept for two days."

Liang patted the doctor on the shoulder as she passed her, heading for the small break room, where she found cups and an assortment of teas, none of which were the kind she really wanted. She chose an herbal with citrus, hoping the antioxidants would give Okalani a boost. The last thing they needed was their doctor come down sick, too.

She heated water, and then poured the steaming liquid over the tea bags. The gentle aroma rose from the cups as she carried them into the office.

"I'll have to bring you some of my personal stock," she said. "My teacher Roddi took the time to instruct me on the use of native herbs to promote health and treat disease. I've made some very creative combinations."

"Thanks." Okalani sipped the brew, winning points with Liang for not asking for sweetener.

Actually, though Liang had taken an immediate dislike to the runaway bride when Captain Rogers had first brought her aboard, practically stealing her from her fiancé, they had since become good friends. Both had been propositioned often by male crewmembers, and they compared notes on how they had turned down the offers. She knew Okalani was holding out for the captain's affection.

Once upon a time she might have criticized the doctor's dreams. Now Liang's outlook on love was shaded in rosy tones. Long protected from unwanted advances, her heart had been stolen by a member of the crew. They had kept their liaison secret so far, just to keep the appearance of professional distance. But she didn't know how long she could keep that feeling of first love from bursting right through her.

Her personal life was irrelevant at the moment, of course. She turned her attention to Okalani's investigation. "It seems significant that only those from the captain's original crew have been affected."

Okalani nodded. "Agreed. I'd thought at first it might be something they'd brought with them from their universe, but further study has shown that's not exactly right. Hal's cells show a large increase in free radicals in the cells, particularly in the mitochondria. This could be a sign of exposure to certain kinds of radiation." She frowned. "Kinds I haven't really seen in my studies here. Certainly nothing we've had on the ship."

"You've reviewed Dr. Montgomery's records?"

"I have. Nothing matches this sort of damage. Especially nothing in the standard files on Bricasterians. So if it's not here, and not there—" She hesitated and gave a deep sigh.

Something totally unexpected popped into Liang's mind. "What if it's neither? What if something that happened *during* the crossover, itself? Something inside the wormhole?"

Okalani's eyes took on a hopeful light for the first time. "That could be it."

"That would explain why only those who'd been there have been affected." A rush of energy zipped through Liang, excitement that they might have a handle on the situation.

"It's been so long, though," the doctor mused. "What would cause a year's delay in this damage?" She took a stylus from her desk and made some notes on a datapad.

"Kai has a collection of data gathered during the passage through the wormhole. I can review his records for comparison radiation readings." Liang drank some tea, thinking. "Perhaps the other artifacts of the Ancients have similar—" Having second thoughts, she paused. "No. We gathered most of those parts here, on Lennor and Terza. If they carried contaminants, those of us from this universe would have become ill."

"Unless it requires a combination of the two. Whatever was gathered during the crossover and exposure to the local artifacts."

Something about that didn't sit right with Liang's logic, but for now it was the only lead they had. "Our pathogen killed an alien member before the humans. So perhaps humans have some resistance."

"But Tasiq is also alien, and he's been asymptomatic."

"Curious." Liang glanced over at the medical beds and their silent occupants. Now one of the Muuvos, Nev, tended to the sick women, checking their life signs. "You should get some sleep."

"I've got to start testing Temms and the others. Maybe I can catch this early in them before they're incapacitated." Okalani stretched, the dark circles under her eyes more pronounced in the artificial light of the infirmary.

Liang stood, taking Okalani's arm. "You'll make better decisions if you're rested. The tests will wait till morning." She gently tugged the other woman to her feet. "I'm sure Nev can handle things here. Unless you wish me to remain in your stead."

Okalani's green eyes widened and she patted Liang's hand on her arm. "No. No reason for you to stay here. Of course, you're right. I'm sure morning is plenty of time. Just in case we're wrong, we should all keep our immune systems as healthy as possible, agreed?"

"Such is my thought."

Okalani suddenly hugged her tight, catching her off guard. She stiffened in surprise, but forced herself to relax, not wanting to upset the already stressed doctor.

"Thanks so much for coming down. I've been so worried about this! I know there's nothing I could have done differently, but I really think I'm letting everyone down. I've just got to find out what the cause of this is so we can eradicate it. Temms is all caught up with this war he's about to start."

She clung to Liang, her body shaking with sobs.

Release was what she needed. What they all needed from time to time. Though Liang had never been much of a hugger, she patted the doctor's back for comfort and let her cry it out. It would bring her better sleep and they had both get started again on the puzzle in the morning.

When the flood of Okalani's tears subsided, Liang released her.

"If I think of anything else, I'll let you know," she said. "Good night."

The doctor managed a faint smile. "Good night, and thank you, my friend."

"It is my pleasure." She nodded to Nev and left the infirmary, her brain still spinning with questions. At least they had made some headway. Tomorrow was another day. Hopefully, without anyone else getting sick.

She made her way to her own small quarters, slowing as she sensed someone waiting outside her door. She peeked around the corner of the corridor, and then found a smile as she recognized who lounged on the wall next to her door.

"Do you usually stalk someone's room in the middle of thirdturn?" she asked Nim Williams.

The security man grinned and reached out as she approached him, gently snaring her arm and pulling her close. "I do when she doesn't answer her comm." He cupped her chin and tilted her head up, looking into her eyes. "Where in blazes were you at this time of night?"

She caressed his close-shaved cheek. "The infirmary."

He released her, a frown sitting on his lips. "Are you sick? Do you have it? What they had?"

"No, of course not. I was just helping Okalani with some research." She took his hand. "We might be making some headway." She explained their latest theory.

His brown eyes sparkled with curiosity. "So Chief Rogers could come down with this disease?"

Liang pursed her lips. "In theory, but I hope we'll solve this mystery first."

He laughed. "Oh, come on, Liang. He's the captain's son. How else will I ever get promoted?"

Before she could become too shocked, he gathered her into his arms and kissed her. "I'm only teasing. The Chief does a fine job. Keeps me off the crappy diplomatic assignments."

She melted into his embrace. In the ship's competitions, she had often noticed his athletic skills and strong muscles. It hadn't taken long before she imagined them interacting with her body, fantasies she never before experienced. He apparently felt the same.

"Before I went to the infirmary, I had another of those dreams. With Roddi and the device."

He continued to hold her tightly, comforting her, stroking her hair as her head lay on his shoulder. "If you let me spend the night with you, I'd keep you safe, Liang. You know I'd never let anything happen to you."

"I know," she murmured.

"So?"

"We can't. Not yet. I'm first officer. I have to—"

He bent his head to kiss her. She thought she would lose herself in the simple touch of his insistent lips, the way her heart sped up, and every part in her body tingled. Waves of desire ran through her, exquisite torture that she wanted to stop and she never wanted to end, all at once.

"You have to what?" he asked, his whisper hot against her ear. "Come on, Liang. Third-turn is half over, and no one's looking. I'll be gone before first-turn. Just let me protect you tonight so you can get some sleep."

He sounded so reasonable, and her head was spinning. If she were honest with herself, she had to admit she wanted nothing less than him in her bed, his arms around her.

I'm a grown woman. Why can't I choose to do what I want just once, instead of always thinking of the ship?

She conceded, a long, shuddering sigh escaping her. "All right. Just tonight."

His smile celebrated victory. "We'll start with tonight," he said. "If you feel safer, maybe we can turn it into a regular thing."

"Hush," she scolded, feeling wicked and elated at the same time. Taking a glance down both directions of the corridor, she saw no one was watching. She keyed in her code, and the door slid open. Still holding his hand, she drew him inside.

He had never been inside her quarters, and he complimented its simple color scheme in earth tones of brown and green, its only décor small bits of natural objects she had acquired in her travels, shells, dried flowers and the like. Her bed was covered with a hand-woven blanket in the soft beige color of desert sands that she had bartered for on their last stop in the gypsies' bazaar on Terza. It was all the home she had left.

He took off his boots, his eyes on her. Her heart beat so fast, she thought it would rattle out of her chest. In the weeks since she had acknowledged her attraction to the handsome Nim, they had only stolen minutes here or an hour there. They had never spent a night together. She had never been with a man all night, ever. Was she ready?

"Liang," he said softly, "I care deeply for you. I wouldn't hurt you. I meant what I said. You sleep. I'll watch and chase away the evil spirits."

He beckoned her close, and slipped off her jacket and her heavy uniform shirt. "Get comfortable, and I'll join you."

Liang noticed every detail of his gentle touch, the way his fingers lingered on her skin. Her logic, her usual ruler by which she judged situations, failed her in this circumstance. She had to go with her intuition, and her intuition told her to trust him. She slipped off her boots, and then her slacks, not looking to see if he watched her. Then she climbed into bed, pulling the sheet and blanket over her.

He entered the bed behind her, under the blankets, still wearing his undershirt and uniform pants. Wiggling close, he slipped an arm under her neck and pulled her back against his chest, his other hand smoothing the hair from her brow. He kissed the top of her head.

"Now, don't worry about a thing. You're safe with me."

Nervous at first, she came to find his presence reassuring. She cuddled up against him and closed her eyes.

"No pressure, love," he whispered. "Just peace."

He reached behind to extinguish the light.

Her conscience scolded her for missing her nightly exercise routine, but she silenced its protests. Instead she set herself to fully experience the moment she was in, the feel of Nim with her, the strength of his embrace, the depth of his protection of her. Within a few minutes, their breaths came into synchronicity. She released herself to fate, praying, as always, to wake with more insight.

Instead of the trouble dreams of her old teacher, or her worries about the illness taking their crew members, she found that for the first night in many, many nights, she slept without disturbance, in perfect safety. The spectre of death didn't haunt her dreams. Even though Nim was gone when she woke, as he had promised, she could sense his presence there still. She felt secure. For an eighteen-year-old girl who had lost her parents, lost her teacher, lost her past, nearly lost her life after the misconduct of her former captain, just the simple feeling that this day she would be fine was a revelation.

And perhaps just the first of many more.

CHAPTER 10

ACTING on one of the solid agreements that had finally emerged from the captains' summit meeting at Roandock, Temms and C. T. Dutton set out to canvass some of the less scrupulous business owners.

The group had assigned teams to check out several potential avenues. First, find out which dealers would support a blockade or boycott of the Agency edicts. Second, discover the Agency loyalists who were then to be avoided at all costs. Third, scout out potential clues to the location of the invisible station.

Temms had tried to backburner that last issue, already dealing with the mystery illness aboard his ship and the brouhaha over the Agency demands. But he couldn't. The dream messages gnawed at his resolve. The fact that he mistrusted the Agency on almost every point made their interest in the object something to be concerned about.

So here they were, downtown in the city. The main street was busy with the rush of after-work pedestrians. Roandock's wide walkways allowed for ample foot traffic, though most of those trying to get from one side of the city to another opted for public transportation. Marriel wasn't as industrialized as the third and fourth planets in the system, Terza and Perpetra, and consequently individually owned transports were expensive and out of favor.

Too many people milling through the streets for his personal comfort, that was for sure.

"Too bad you couldn't get Kyndra to come lean on these people. It would save a lot of talking," Temms said to C. T., only half joking.

"*She* chooses her assignments. Not me."

The statement was definitive. Sounded like he had tried to recruit Kyndra one too many times and had gotten burned.

"Just a thought, friend. No criticism implied. If the Ancients are broadcasting this information and the Agency's looking, I'd think this would be more common knowledge. Someone's got to know more than they're saying. We just haven't found the right one yet."

C. T. slowed to walk alongside him. "You keep telling me about these dreams, Temms. How the Ancients speak directly to you about the missing piece of the station, asking for your help. I've got to ask, don't you think that's a little strange? You, out of the millions of people in this universe?"

Stung, Temms frowned and ducked aside as he was nearly marched over by a pair of broad-shouldered, jaundice-skinned aliens. "What's wrong with me?"

C. T. raised his hands in surrender. "I'm not saying anything's wrong. But it's odd as hell. Kyndra's normally a real sensitive when it comes to these things, and she's felt nothing. You heard the group when we met— no one's looking at this as more than a rumor. Yet you're convinced. Is there anyone else on your ship that's having the same dreams?"

"I, uh, I haven't asked. Maybe I will."

C. T. clapped him on the shoulder. "Maybe you should. You've got to remember that you aren't carrying your load all by yourself, Temms. You've got a fine crew and friends out here in the void ready to stand by you. It'll come when the time's right, and you've got enough information."

He yanked Temms aside as a wheeled rickshaw barreled past, too close to the curb.

"Right now, all you know is that there's a thing and it's hidden by someone. Not a lot to go on, you know?"

"Fine, fine," Temms muttered. These thoughts weren't any different than those haunting his own mind.

If I could just get a handle on one of the crises, maybe the rest would fall into line.

He checked the time. Enough to meet with one more business owner before rendezvous with Liang and Valeni Pascual at Jowalt Edwards' place. They continued down the street to the pawn shop run by an old associate of C. T.'s. Temms let C. T. take the lead on this one, since he knew exactly how to play the grizzled owner, who kept the household goods on the counters out front and the illicit arms in the back closets. It was a brief encounter, the dealer terse and disinterested, especially on the subject of the Agency.

"You're messing in places you don't want to be, C. T." The dealer shot Temms a hostile look. "Just straighten up. Things'll work out fine."

C. T. thanked his friend and then left without further argument. Temms was even more convinced that nothing at all would work out fine.

After that disappointing last round, they still had some time before he met up with the teams he had brought to the planet, Liang and Valeni from the *Six-Shooter,* and Gretta Flan and one of his newest recruits from Sol Aeris. Needing a moment to relax and regroup, Temms and C. T.

retired to the Flaming Flagon for something sufficiently alcoholic to tend to their mental wounds. When they were pleasantly ensconced in a corner table of the poorly-lit, dark-paneled saloon, Temms took a long drink of honey ale. He savored its dry aftertaste, letting it take his mind away from his frustration.

The patrons around them gathered, laughed, and drank, lost in their handheld gaming devices, as the wagers rose and fell. It was as if they had no concerns about the power of the omnipresent Agency, and no interest in changing the priorities of their world financial regime.

"As long as they have their indi-games to blot out their day-to-day reality," he muttered, "they don't care about the big evil that touches their every purchase, their every breath."

"You mean the Agency? Evil is a little strong, wouldn't you say? It's an inconvenience, to be sure, but one that's a usual necessity. If it wasn't the Agency, it would be the government, taxing us to raise money for the common good."

Temms leaned in, his elbows on the edge of the wooden table. "But at least it would be for the common good then. What does the Agency provide? Nothing except a bureaucratic headache and a threat of violence to those who don't roll over and surrender."

C. T. studied him over his half-empty glass.

"Your obsession isn't about the Agency, is it, Temms? Not really. We've all had to deal with government or its arms digging into our pockets. But you're not willing to let go of it. Something else feels like it's at work here."

Temms eyed him. Was that Kyndra's determination, or just a wild guess? No question it was true. The heavy-handed tactics of the Agency reminded Temms of the very worst of the Confederation. But he could separate the two. Surely he could.

"It feels personal. Like they've singled me out for some reason. They came to meet with me on my ship. Have they gone around having tea with anyone else?"

C. T. shrugged. "Not that I know of. But you're new. Maybe they just needed a fresh victim."

His lips drew tight into a line. "I don't sit well with that role."

"I can understand that." The other man eyed Temms, contemplating, and then finished off his ale. "Maybe they believe in your connection with this muddle of the Ancients. If you're the only one having communication with them, it would be logical for them to follow you."

"Yeah? Well I could stand being a little less special. All I want is to be able to get back to business."

C. T. waved the server close to order another round. "I'm not much of a mystic, Temms, but I've learned over the years that all you can do is keep your mind open to possibilities. If you're meant to discover the great answers of the universe, they'll come to you."

Was C. T. patronizing him? Temms eyed his companion, thinking they were better friends than that. "Yeah." He took a long drink of the new ale the server set down as she passed. "If I manage to learn all that, I'll buy myself a turban and open a booth in the marketplace, telling fortunes."

C. T. laughed. "That would be something to see, mate."

The comment changed the path of the conversation to lighter topics, and they spent a quarter hour finishing their ale. Temms finally glanced at his timepiece. "Time to go." He drained his glass and left some coins on the table, giving the curvaceous server a farewell wave.

Outside, the two men headed in the direction of Jowalt Edward's gritty little shop, where they had agreed to meet the others.

"She was a looker."

Temms twitched. "Who?"

"That waitress. I saw her wink when we sat down."

"So?"

"So." He laughed. "It's nice to see you relax a little, my friend. You're such a man on a mission. More to life than evil and conspiracies, isn't there?"

C. T.'s tone was light, but something in it got under Temms' skin. He relaxed—often, by hells fire. Why was everyone always nagging him about his dedication? He wasn't the only one who would benefit if the Agency lost some of its overreaching power. He was looking out for the interests of all the captains in their merry little band. His own leisure could wait.

CHAPTER 11

SILENTLY fuming, he allowed his annoyance to flow through him, spurring his pace.

By the time they had traveled the several blocks to their destination, he had released the tendency to snap. The door creaked open, but no bell announced their entry. Inside, shadowy shelves were loaded with used ship parts and other mechanicals, the grimy front counter unmanned. Dust motes hovered in the air, lit by the diffuse sunlight that streaked through the storefront window. The dim interior smelled of burnt oil and old must. Didn't Jowalt ever stop to sweep out the place?

A narrow glance through the door into the back room showed him the wiry mechanic arguing with Temms' petite first officer. Their faces were flushed and muscles stiff as they faced each other, glaring. Valeni stood apart from them, arms crossed, one eyebrow raised as she watched Liang.

"Looks like trouble," Temms muttered.

C. T. hung back, eyes narrowed. "Should we let them settle it before we go in?"

"You're asking for a death sentence!" Jowalt yelled, slamming his fist on his cluttered work table. "You know better than this. You can't back him against the Agency."

Temms hesitated. "Maybe we'll learn more this way." He stepped out of the direct light from the door.

"What do you care, Jowalt?" Liang shot back. Her tone sparked like an electric warning fence.

Jowalt reached for her, but she ducked back away from him.

His voice dropped, becoming almost soft. "I care, Chen. I care."

He cares for my Liang?

Temms stiffened. She had never said anything about that. But her wide eyes and dropped jaw tended to militate against any such feelings on her part.

Silence hung between them until Valeni finally stepped in.

"Look, we're not going to resolve anything here. The question was, do you know anything about this station. Is your answer no?" She pinned Jowalt with her stare.

The skinny grease monkey pulled the black-smeared headband off his forehead and tossed it onto the pile of trash behind him, and then wiped his face on his sleeve. "You can't seriously expect me to speak out against the organization that audits my books. If they shut me down, I could be out of business overnight."

"Coward," Liang said under her breath.

Temms coughed discreetly, and all three of them looked up, startled.

"Sorry to interrupt," he said, joining them in the back room, C. T. on his heels. "I understand your reluctance, Jowalt. The Agency has supreme power. I'd obviously like to change that, for the protection of everyone." He shrugged, his gaze locked with the mechanic's. "But we're not looking for this thing to turn it over to them. We want to—"

Jowalt rolled his dark eyes. "Yeah, I know what you want. You want to harvest the artifacts and build yourself a super-weapon."

Temms couldn't have been more surprised if Jowalt Edwards had punched him in the face. "I—what?"

"Don't be ridiculous!" Liang snapped.

Jowalt's gaze darted from one of them to the other like a vole hyped up on speed. "That's what the scuttlebutt says. You hunted down a gob of those artifacts already, and you used them to destroy an empire where you came from. You're looking for these so you can challenge the Agency and you're going to destroy the worlds."

A shocked silence settled over the room at his pronouncement. Then C. T. started laughing.

"All this time I've been associating with a destroyer of worlds, and I didn't even know it? Wonderful! Hey, Temms, why haven't you just singlehandedly blown up Agency headquarters by now?" His eyes twinkled with merriment.

Temms was still knee deep in astonishment. "I don't see what's so funny."

C. T. made an exaggerated courtly bow. "Your reputation precedes you, my liege. Clearly this explains why the Agency is so focused on your ship and its captain."

Temms raised an eyebrow, assimilating the information in its proper perspective, despite C. T.'s annoying presentation. That had to be it. The Agency knew, through its association with Commander Burko, that Temms had access to the artifacts from the other universe.

He hadn't internalized the fact it was apparently common knowledge. So when he had sought out those artifacts held by the council on Lennor or the others he had found, he hadn't broadcast the fact generally. But he also hadn't made a secret that he was seeking pieces of the Ancients' work to complete the machine Monty and Benzi eventually built.

But it was never intended as a super-weapon. Or any weapon at all, really.

They didn't know that for sure.

How did Jowalt know?

He studied Liang's outraged expression, Valeni's wry amusement. Better squash this rumor right now.

"Look, Mr. Edwards, I have no intention of blowing up anything. Anything at all." Temms took a step forward. "I'm just here to hunt down the possibilities that the Ancients left more wisdom to share with us all. It's a miracle that they exist, and that their artifacts might teach us something we need to exist in this uni—in our daily lives."

No sense in giving away their foreign status, in case there was anyone who still didn't know it.

"Yeah," C. T. interjected. "And if the Agency gets to it first, they'll take it for themselves, just like they have everything else. No one else will benefit from it. Do you suppose the Ancients left this information, these miracles, for only the Agency?"

Jowalt retreated behind his jumbled work table. "You know what? I own this business, shabby as it is. If I'm lucky, I make enough to send home to feed my ma and my brothers. I don't ask questions about stuff that don't concern me. I just pay my tariffs and move on. Whatever you want to do, pal, feel free. Just leave me out of it."

"Fine." Temms wasn't too disappointed. He expected resistance. The Agency had been top dog on the inner planets for a long time. "Let's go, people."

Valeni shrugged and brushed dust off her jacket. "The sooner we get fresh air the better." She slid past Temms in a cloud of floral perfume, continuing out the door. C. T. followed her.

"Have a good day, Mr. Edwards," Temms said. "Liang?"

"I'll be there in a minute," she said.

A little sting of surprise ran through the captain, but he nodded. "All right. We'll be outside."

He went outside, out of habit taking a long look up and down the street in case someone was spying on him, but no one seemed to notice their presence. Through the window, he could see Liang and Jowalt in agitated conversation, accompanied by angry gestures.

Valeni leaned close. "She's got the best chance to get the information you're looking for. Just leave her to it."

"Really?" Temms frowned. "They don't really have a—I mean,

anything between…." He trailed off, noting again that sometimes he was blind to things right under his nose. Just as Tommy was growing up, Liang was too. He considered her more his daughter than his own Linz had ever been.

She can do better than this Jowalt guy.

As Liang slapped her hand on the dirty table and then headed for the door, he decided he didn't have anything to worry about.

Valeni laughed. "As long as he still thinks he has a chance to convert her, she can string him along. She'll get something out of him, eventually."

"He seems pretty determined."

"Oh, Captain, don't be so naïve. Women have the gift of a way to wiggle inside a man's defenses." Valeni smiled. "Nikki's taught me much about the powers of a woman. Trust me."

Her eyes shone up into his, rich chocolate-toned pools of light, and Temms had to drag himself back out of them. "If you say so."

Liang marched up to them, giving Valeni a once-over. "We're done here," she said.

"Let's go, then." Temms made sure they were all together and then led them down the alley toward the place he had parked the slipcraft. They would return to the ship without the information they had come for. It wasn't a loss—yet.

The station was still out there. He would find it, along with its missing parts, sooner or later.

Until then he had his people to look out for. Hopefully no more of them would be sick by the time he returned.

The four proceeded down the squalid street lined with low-rent storefronts toward the rendezvous point. C. T. seemed almost morose, walking along, hands in his jacket pockets, eyes on the horizon. Valeni, too, felt distracted, not quite present. Temms maneuvered closer to Liang, who strode along as if her boots were afire.

"What was that all about?" he asked.

"Jowalt being an ass?" she replied, staring at the ground as she marched.

Her unaccustomed pejorative raising an eyebrow, he hurried to keep up. "That, too. I suppose the man's entitled to his opinion about the Agency and the artifacts. Even if he's misinformed."

"He expects me to betray my captain! It's an insult to my character."

"It sounded more to me like he was worried about you, Liang. For whatever reason—"

She whirled around to face him, cutting him off with a hot stare. "I have never given that rodent the slightest reason to believe he could hope to win me. And I never will."

Her righteous indignation was so adorable, it was all Temms could do to keep from smiling. Then the shooting started.

Laser fire shot out of an alley ahead of them, and he yanked Liang aside, pushing her behind a large metal trash container.

"Take cover!" he yelled, snatching his laser pistol from its holster.

Valeni hit the ground with a shoulder roll that took her inside a doorway.

He couldn't see C. T., but knew he had to be close.

Gretta Flan came flying out of the alley at a dead run, shots echoing behind her. Her pale lavender hair, usually piled neatly on her head, was disheveled and swinging loose. Blood graced her left cheek.

Temms stepped out far enough for her to see him, beckoning her in behind the container. Gasping for breath, she diverted her path and came to join them.

Two rough-looking men came running out of the alley after her. Neither was Temms' other crew member. One held a long machete-style knife, and the other had pistols in each hand. The second one aimed in Gretta's direction and pulled the trigger. The bullet ricocheted off the building behind them and pinged against the back of the container.

"Drop it!" C. T. appeared from a doorway behind the two men, his own large firearm drawn.

Surprised, the first man's knife arm dropped to his side. The second man apparently felt lucky, and drew a bead on C. T.

"What are you gonna do, old man? Shoot me?"

Temms didn't hesitate, but fired at the man's gun arm, just above the elbow. "I will if he won't."

The ruffian yelped as the laser burned him, dropping the gun. He swayed, and then pulled the other up to fire at Temms. Valeni fired then, a red bloom appearing where the man's left wrist used to be.

C. T. stared at the other man until he dropped the machete. Weaponless, he ducked back into the alley, his footsteps slapping against the stones, dwindling into the distance.

The teams converged on the wounded man, who had fallen to his knees, bleeding.

Still out of breath, Gretta came up behind Temms, her eyes hard. "They ambushed us just off Pyger Court," she said. "Said they knew we were part of your crew, and we needed to be taught a lesson."

She aimed a kick at the man. "He tried to grab me, no doubt what he intended. Bob tried to stop him." Her throat caught, and she barely got the rest of the words out. "The other one hacked at him with that knife and—and I think he's dead." Tears flowed down her bloody cheek. Valeni slipped a supporting arm around Gretta's shoulders. "I'm so sorry, Captain. I left him because I knew I'd be next!"

Temms' anger boiled up inside like someone had lit a rocket engine in his gut. He pointed his weapon right at the man's filthy face. "What in the hells did you attack my people for? What have we ever done to you?"

The man turned slowly to glare up at Temms. "You'd best watch yourself. They's put out a reward for makin' your life difficult, Captain Fancy Rogers. Work's not easy to come by here in Roandock, 'cause of blighters like you, screwing with the powers that be. Men got to feed their families. Agency's gonna pay, they're gonna take it."

C. T. stole a look over his shoulder.

"He's probably right, Temms. We'd best get ourselves off the street and back up to our ships. If word gets around that we're here...."

He trailed off, and the man on his knees just smiled.

Temms wanted nothing more than to wipe that smug smirk off his face, or more realistically, to smash in the side of his head. So the Agency thought sending street thugs after him was the way to make him cave? They were sorely mistaken.

"All right. Come on."

He shoved the fallen man aside, and he landed on his face in the street. Temms kicked the weapons out of reach, and then hurried the small group down the alley in the direction the men had come. He didn't intend to leave his officer behind.

Gretta led them back to the point where Bob had been attacked. From the amount of blood that had pooled around him on the ground, there was no doubt he was dead.

From there, it was a blur as Temms steeled himself to do what had to be done. He slung the dead man over his shoulder and carried him, that fire still burning inside, all the way back to the place their slipcraft awaited. Liang helped get him aboard, Gretta starting to fall apart by then. Valeni and C. T. left in one of the *Fuego*'s small craft.

With a last look around, Temms closed up the hatch and took the pilot's seat. The day had been a total waste, and he had lost a man. The Agency had stepped over the line. No more diplomacy. As far as he was concerned, they had declared war.

CHAPTER 12

BENZI Quinn surveyed the engineering section from the upper level where Dani's desk awaited her return from the infirmary.

If only she would come back.

As days and weeks passed with both the gregarious Dani Jamar and good-natured Halian missing, the department held a different vibration, a physical lack that was starting to drag on the remaining members as the days passed. Though he would deny it to anyone who asked. Especially about the alien. Everyone knew how Benzi felt about aliens.

But damned if I don't miss him every day.

Benzi paced on the deck, staring down at the activity on the main level, especially the cataloguing operation that was taking place on the large conglomeration of work tables in the back. The captain had a fire burning under a project involving the Ancients' artifacts.

Though they had disassembled both the first machine built in the old universe, the one that created the wormhole that got them here, and the second one that had sent Rogers' enemies home, their equipment permanently damaged, some new imperative had arisen. He had ordered a current inventory at the earliest time possible.

"Wouldn't it be fine if the Cap would fill me in on why, just once in awhile?" Benzi muttered.

"Hey, chief? Give us a hand?" Iov called from below.

More wogs, that's what Rogers gave him. Iov and his younger brother Uri both worked engineering shifts now. At least they were built like humans. Mostly. If they wore long sleeves to hide their striped arms, just their large eyes gave them away as aliens. So far, though, they seemed pretty healthy. He hoped they wouldn't succumb to whatever had taken Halian.

'Cause I need a full crew. Not 'cause I care.

"Coming." Benzi pulled a billed cap on his head and clanked down the metal steps to the main floor of engineering. "What's holding up the—oh."

So that's why they had called him.

Monty sat on a tall stool next to the work table, a pile of the copper-colored metal artifacts in front of him. A high-pitched humming came from his lips as he manipulated the pieces, trying to fit them together.

"Whatcha making, snapper?"

Since Monty had come to him ten months before, a damaged boy abandoned on the ship by some well-meaning aliens, he had gradually been tamed from a feral child who bit and scratched, to a boy who escaped into flights of engineering feats. He could do some wonderful things, so Benzi hated to shut him down, but when he got in the way, it was an issue.

Benzi came closer, moving slowly so as not to spook the boy. The eyes of everyone on the unit followed Benzi, making him feel like a target on a laser range.

"Need power," Monty mumbled. Sweaty dark bangs hung over his eyes. Shoulders hunched, his fingers twisted at the metal pieces with frantic speed. He hadn't been sleeping well, dreams waking him many times a night, though he could never explain them to Benzi any further than "someone asking too many questions." His lack of sleep led to more erratic behavior. Like this.

If it didn't stop soon, he would have to consult with the doc.

But she's got enough on her tray for now.

"What kind of power?" Benzi glanced over the items on the table. "We have stored batteries. Will that do?"

"What's he making?" Iov asked, eyes even bigger and blacker than usual as he stared at the boy.

"No idea." He pulled a stool up to the boy. "Will batteries help?"

Monty put his head down on his arms on the table. "Have to connect. Have to find her."

"Who are you looking for, snapper? Dani's in the infirmary. She'll be back soon."

Benzi gestured to Uri, who hung back by the light panel. "Get me some batteries. Four or more. Take one of the cart baskets."

The brightly-dressed Muuvo grabbed a metal cargo basket and disappeared through the doorway that led down to the engine room.

"Not Dani. Her. The shining one." Monty continued to fiddle with the pieces. Benzi couldn't detect a pattern in any of the combinations he made. The parts he obsessed over were some of those the women had collected in the underground caves of Lennor, some the crew had retrieved from the burnt panels of the *Doubtful* after its passage from the wormhole, and some Benzi didn't recognize at all.

"That's not very helpful, son. Can you try again?"

The boy just shook his head, refocused on the pieces again.

Benzi studied the boy and then the pieces, waiting for the magic illumination, the rush of power that he and Monty had been able to create the last time all the pieces had been put together, but nothing happened. Even after thick-bodied Uri brought the batteries and offered them to Monty, nothing changed.

Finally Benzi stood and pushed himself away from the table. "He won't hurt anything, Iov. Just let him be. When he's agitated like this, it's best to let him focus and work it out." He studied Monty again and then sighed. "Come on, people, back to work. Lot to do to keep this whole ship running." He patted the boy on the head. "Don't work yourself sick, snap. I'll come get you at end of watch."

As the others drifted back to their duties, Benzi wiped his forehead, feeling overwhelmed. Being chief didn't mean he ran the department. Without Dani's steady hand, he felt more of that responsibility falling on his shoulders. He had been happy with the position Rogers had given him, even though he might not have realized it before.

He wanted Dani back. He needed her.

He made a mental note to visit the infirmary at shift's end to get an update, perhaps sit with Dani Jamar and tell her how necessary she was to everyday life in the engineering deck of the *Doubtful*. Maybe she would hear him. Maybe she would come back from the steps outside death's door and everything would get back to normal. Or as normal as it ever got around here.

"If my luck runs better than usual," he muttered, and went back to his office.

CHAPTER 13

LIANG Chao returned to the ship, the events of the day burned into her mind.

The death of an officer hurt them all, and she struggled with his loss. The captain had called for a team to take the body to the morgue and Gretta to the infirmary for her wounds to be treated. When had everything gotten so out of control?

And what in all the stars was wrong with Jowalt? Sure, he had tried to contact her multiple times over the months since Kevan had dumped her and Rogers had rescued her. At first he had come up with pretexts, some item he was certain the *Doubtful* could use. Later, the calls became more personal, asking when the ship might come to Roandock. Or whether she needed anything he could send her from groundside. She never encouraged him. She had always thought he was just harassing her.

Maybe that was what had blindsided her so brilliantly when he burst into a rant protesting her work with Captain Rogers, and then followed it with a declaration of his feeling for her.

As if I could care for that dirty-dealing grease monkey. I'd sooner bed Benzi Quinn.

The thought of either alternative sent shudders down her spine. Action. That's what she needed. Sustained, heart-pumping action, to flush the images from her system.

She checked in at the bridge, and then retreated to the ship's gym, running through the katas she had learned from Roddi in her school days. The long-practiced routines soothed her mind and body. As the time passed, she jacked up the intensity, increasing the difficulty of the exercises until everything was motion, nothing was thought.

Her arms tightened as she moved into a handspring, launching into the air to land on her hands, and then rotating back to the vertical again, landing with her hands to the right, defensively positioned near her face. She immediately spun and went into a series of kicks, moving progressively closer to the exit, the last one bringing her nearly to the gym door, which swung open as she landed.

The surprise of the sudden movement sent her off balance, and she would have fallen if Nim Williams hadn't grabbed her arm.

"Hey, watch out there." His grin was soft and appealing. "Didn't mean to startle you."

She gently untangled her arm from his and backed away from the door. "No harm done."

"What's after you?" He came into the room and looked back toward the locker facility. "You look like you're ready for a fight."

She shrugged. The last thing she wanted to do was tell him about Jowalt. "You heard what happened on the planet?"

"Damned Agency goons. I never thought they'd have the balls to come after us direct like that. See, I thought Rogers should have sent security people down to do his scouting, not communications officers. Gretta's not equipped to deal with that kind of fight."

Liang had wondered on that point herself, but Gretta's role hadn't really occurred to her. "She graduated in your class, right? Didn't they teach self-defense to everyone?"

"Of course, but we specialized in it." Nim cocked his head. "Unless you're thinking she let her partner get killed."

"What? No." The thought froze her. Bob had his quirks, but in the intra-ship games, he had always held his own. "He should have been able to handle the situation."

Nim caught her gaze in the mirror beside them. "You don't think she's working with the Agency, do you? That it was a set-up?"

"Gretta? That isn't possible. The captain has trusted her with the most private of ship's communications." She tried to shake off the icy chill that threatened to set into her bones. "She wouldn't betray him that way."

His jaw tightened, and he nodded. "You're right, love. He's given each of us an opportunity that's special. There's no reason to suspect her." A sheepish grin came to him. "You know security guys. We tend to over-think and be paranoid."

"I know." She stretched. "I wanted to come in here to work off some stress and stop thinking for awhile."

"Can I play?"

His demeanor lightened, eyes now sparkling with mischief, and he moved into a defensive posture, feet planted firmly and arms raised to block. She knew he was a good fighter. It was one of the things that had appealed to her most about him. Maybe this was just what she needed to wipe Jowalt's ridiculousness from her mind, and the horror from the day in general. A faint answering smile crept onto her lips.

"If you think you can keep up."

A plan of attack formed in a split second, and she came at him with a roundhouse kick, ducking quickly away from his attempt to grab her ankle, recovering with a quick shot to the head and a kick to his midsection. They circled the room, trading feints, making an occasional connection. Then she let herself sink low, out of the reach of his long arms, before turning into a handspring, letting her foot catch him square on the shoulder, making him stumble backward.

He retaliated with a series of short shots with his fists aimed at her head and shoulders that she easily blocked, but when she had been seduced by his rhythm, he twisted and put a knee in her back. Catching her when she would have fallen, he dropped to his knees and pulled her near, their faces inches apart, both breathing hard after the intense exertion. "Had enough?" he asked softly.

He leaned closer, and she thought he might kiss her. Then he did.

A moment later, he stood, pulling her upright with him, and then spun her away toward the wall. When she recovered, she found him ready for round two.

"If that's how you want to play it, mister," she teased, and she launched into an attack. They sparred across the room and back, well-matched in rhythm and speed, until he managed to grab her wrist, pulling her back against his chest, an arm across her throat just tightly enough that she couldn't escape.

"Do you surrender, princess?" he asked.

"I never surrender."

"We'll see about that."

His breath was hot against her ear. His free hand moved along the front of her body, starting at her waist and moving slowly, so slowly toward her breasts. When they finally touched her there, the emotion and desire she felt was so strong, she thought she would faint.

Then the door opened.

Nim and Liang stiffened. He brushed her ear with his lips and then released her. She stepped away, trying to control her breath. The glimpse of her face in the mirror across the room found her cheeks flushed, and her eyes very bright. Nim appeared much the same. His eyes met hers with an expression of regret.

Tommy Rogers came into the gym, acting very much like he hadn't seen what just happened.

"Hey, Chief," Nim said, brushing imagined lint from his uniform.

"We're off-duty. Call me Tommy."

The captain's son started coughing as he walked toward the back room, where the rack of free weights was stored. Knowing what she did about Okalani's study of the mystery illness, Liang studied him, a little worried. His face was pale and his forehead sweaty. But he was just coming into the facility.

"Are you feeling all right?" she asked.

"Sure. Just have a little virus or something. With all the coming and going lately, it's to be expected." He shrugged. "Thought I'd come down here and lift some weights to get my blood going and clear this out of my system." He coughed again.

"Perhaps that will succeed." She stepped aside, half standing behind Nim.

"Hope so. You two carry on with…whatever."

"Right." Nim grinned and winked at Liang, but she shook her head. Whatever mood they had established had been shattered by Tommy's arrival. Perhaps it was just as well. She could go back to her quarters and shower, and then put in some research time at the bridge science station.

Tommy continued into the back room, and the clank of weight disks followed soon after. Watching Nim in the mirror, she could see he was disappointed. They had been so careful to hide their relationship, but what difference did it make, really? The captain had never strictly forbidden it. It might have been part of the rules in his long-lost Confederation. But now?

The weights clanked again, but this time in a jangling crash, followed by a wheezing run of coughing.

Nim took off at a run for the back room, and Liang followed. They found Tommy Rogers lying on the floor gasping, the free weights lying in a circle around him.

She hit the intercom button on the wall. "Medical emergency in the gym! Respiratory emergency!"

"On our way."

Liang knelt down next to Tommy, rolling him onto his side. He struggled to breathe, his eyes wide with alarm.

"I've called the doctor. She will be here shortly," she reassured him.

He wheezed his thanks, hand pulling at his chest, trying to sit up.

"Just take it easy, Chief. Stay there till the doc comes," Nim said.

Very soon after, the door flew open and Okalani rushed in, followed by Lavan and a hovermat. Liang stepped back out of their way, her previous calm escaping as they loaded him on the mat, oxygen mask strapped to his face, and disappeared with him.

Stunned by the action of the last several minutes, Liang leaned on the wall behind her. She exchanged looks with Nim, surprised to read guilt in his eyes. Of course. He had practically wished the illness on the captain's son, so he could have a shot at promotion.

"Hey, Liang, I didn't—"

He didn't need to explain. "I know you didn't." She crossed to slip her arms around him, her turn to provide comfort. "But if he's off duty, you'll need to step up." She squeezed him tight, and then released him. "Come on, we both better go."

Murmuring in confusion, he left the gym with her, turning down the left corridor to go to his quarters. Liang continued to hers, running through the list of candidates in her head. Only three others had come from the other universe—Kai Windthorp, Tasiq and Captain Temms Rogers.

Who would be devastated that his son was ill.

Realizing that would be the worst impact of all, Liang quickly showered and changed, and then hurried to the infirmary.

CHAPTER 14

HIS heart pounding, Temms turned off the intercom and sprinted out of his office for the infirmary.

Since Halian had died, the thought had been in the back of his mind that the remainder of the crossover crew could be infected. But he had remained perfectly healthy. He had just assumed that meant Tommy would be healthy, too.

He couldn't lose Tommy. He wouldn't allow it.

He burst through the door to the infirmary, out of breath. Okalani took one look at him and blanched. "No!" she gasped.

"No, what?" Temms stopped, leaning on the door frame. "Where's Tommy?"

She hurried to his side. "Come on, sit down and I'll get you on respiratory help."

"What?" He straightened and looked down at her. "I don't need respiratory. I'm fine."

The doctor stared at him, hand on her medi-scanner. "Are you sure?"

"Yes, I'm sure!" he snapped. "Where's Tommy?"

"Over here," she said, taking his arm, leading him to a makeshift sickbed set up in the storage room behind the main treatment area. His handsome son was almost lost under a breathing mask, a fever reducing cloth across his forehead. Temms' stomach clenched like a fist.

"He's got what they have?"

Okalani nodded. "It's hit him a lot faster." She drew a shuddering breath. "I'm so sorry. I don't know what else we can do."

Overwhelmed, he ran a hand over his forehead and through what was left of his salt and pepper hair. Someone had to do something. What would Heath Montgomery have done? "Maybe we need to set down on Marriel or Terza and find a real medical facility."

Okalani looked hurt for just a moment, and then she nodded. "Maybe we have no choice."

"How can this happen?" Temms growled, pacing, frustration driving his feet. "It's all the crew that came through with me. Right?"

"That's what we've determined. Our working theory is that something affected your cell structure during the wormhole transit.

Halian's mitochondria showed residual damage." She hung her head. "We haven't been able to find anything similar in Dani's or Riviera's cells, however. So it's not definite."

"Damage from the wormhole? A year later? How is that possible?"

He stepped aside as one of the Muuvos came in to change the medication in Tommy's intravenous bag. The alien moved gracefully for his thick form, his meaty fingers performing the delicate task deftly, and then he left the room without comment.

"We're not sure."

Rogers counted off on his fingers. "Riviera, Dani, Hal, Tommy, me, Kai, and Tasiq." He tried to recollect how his navigator and communications officer had seemed when he had last seen them. Healthy enough to be at their posts on the bridge. And he felt just fine. Hardly a muscle ache.

"You're missing something. You have to be." He looked down at his son, and then heard the soft sniffles beside him. Okalani was crying.

"I've let you down, Temms. After all you've done for me." Her shoulders shook and she covered her face with her hands as the tears let loose like a flood.

His arm came up automatically to slide around her shoulders, holding her close. "It's not your fault. If this was something we brought with us, then we're going to find it somewhere in Montgomery's records. Do you need help searching?"

"Liang and I have been through everything we've found. The only part of the records we can't access is a section during the crossover itself. The logs are damaged."

A sharp memory came to Temms of the order he had given to do just that—to secrete and destroy the records so those still loyal to the Confederation didn't discover that he and his officers had been part of the rebel uprising. Had he doomed them by a short-sighted cover-up?

Tommy stirred, moaning as if he was in pain. Helpless to cure him, Temms took his hand for comfort. He just wasn't sure which of them needed the comfort more.

"Don't." She pulled his hand away and gave him a sterile cloth to wipe it. "We can't risk you."

"There's nothing wrong with me. I feel fine." He protested further as Okalani dragged him to a chair next to her desk and sat him down, scanning him with a series of different pieces of equipment.

"Tommy's symptoms manifested abruptly. Yours could, too."

He barely tolerated her intense scrutiny, only sitting in hopes that something she might find would help Tommy and the others.

When she was done, she sighed. "Damn it to the third hell. Nothing. Everything reads perfect."

"See? I told you." He stretched weary shoulders and leaned back in the chair. "What can I do to help your process? Am I immune, do you think? Could you create some sort of cure from my blood?"

Her expression froze, eyes wide, and then her jaw slowly dropped.

"Lani?"

"Immunity." She whirled her chair around to face her desk, tapping on the keys of her computer almost faster than he could follow. He got up and stepped closer, watching over her shoulder as the green letters appeared on her black screen. She listed the symptoms and sent it to some sort of database. A few seconds later, a list of information appeared, scrolling from top to bottom. "Yes!" she cried.

"Yes what?" He studied the words, but they were mostly jargon and in formal medical language he just couldn't understand. "What does it say?"

"That's it." She hit the intership comm. "Liang Chao, Shiro Vered, Zandra Cilka, report to the infirmary immediately!"

She jumped out of her chair, heading for the lab area. Mystified, Temms followed her.

"Please, Lani. What?"

A smile cracked her face at last. "I was so stupid. I was sure that because it was your people that it had to do with you. It may not have. You gave me the clue, immunity." She gathered microscopes, petri dishes and other equipment and set them on a work table. "Eckiner's Syncytium wiped out huge sections of the population of Marriel hundreds of years ago. They managed to find a cure. Then a vaccine. The inoculation was mandatory across the population, because the government didn't want anyone to get it again. No one has, for hundreds of years. We didn't even think of it, it's been so long."

She bustled around the room, shoving him out of the way when she needed to get past, intent on her task.

"All I need to do is confirm that this is the infectious agent causing their illness. I'm sure no one's stored a ready supply of the medicine needed on the planet, because the disease has been effectively eradicated. But we can fabricate enough to handle this outbreak. The records exist for the formulas."

Passing by him again, she stopped long enough to hug him, and gave him a kiss on the lips. "We're gonna beat this thing, Temms. We will."

The door opened and Liang struggled in, Kai Windthorp leaning on her shoulder. He coughed, wheezing, his dark skin glistening with sweat. Liang looked from Okalani to the captain. "Another patient for you."

"That's great!" Okalani said, gesturing to Nev to help Lavan get Kai into bed. They had to set up a second makeshift cot next to Tommy's, as all the infirmary's regular beds were already filled. But with smooth efficiency, they had him lying down, with an oxygen mask to help him breath and intravenous fluids bringing him what palliatives they could provide.

"Great?" Liang asked, rotating her shoulder to loosen it. "That's another sick crewman, Captain. How's Tommy?"

The reminder stabbed through him, but he tried to let the hope Okalani had instilled buoy him up for now. "Not good. But Lani says she's got a fix on the illness. Some kind of echinoderm synthesis or something." He waved his hand vaguely.

"Eckiner's Syncytium," Okalani said as she hurried past, carrying a microscope.

"I have not heard of—Ah," Liang said. "Something that hasn't been an issue here."

"Right," the captain said. He stepped back against the wall as Shiro and Zandra bustled in, making the small room feel very crowded to him. The doctor barked orders at them to get blood samples from all the patients.

"I want analysis immediately. If the results show what I think they will, I'll need the synthesization titrators set up and in operation. We're finding a cure, people. Today."

Liang shared a small smile. "If this is the answer, Tommy will be recovered in no time."

"Thanks for bringing him down. Are you all right?" he asked.

She nodded. "Kai's just a good-sized man. I had to haul him most of the way myself."

Then the doctor called Liang to come help process the samples the techs sent to the lab. Temms had to commend Lani's efficient attitude. He had to believe that if she was right about this, he would have his crew back in a matter of days.

"You go on," he said. "I'm going to sit with Tommy a bit, just for my own peace of mind."

He stepped aside and the rest of them sprang to action, tending patients, taking more samples and bending over their paraphernalia, busily focused on their mission. Feeling well outside his area of expertise, he pulled up a chair on the far side of the unconscious Tommy's bed, sat back and took a moment to pool his own energy. He needed his wits and his full crew about him to present the best front possible against the confrontation with the Agency that would come, sooner or later. *Please, make it later.* They just weren't ready yet.

Kai's breathing evened out as he settled into the cot. Temms caught Kai's anxious look and grinned.

"The doctor has a strong idea and direction on this thing, Kai. Don't worry."

Kai's gaze was troubled. "Do I have what—what Halian died of?"

Temms recognized the tone of soldiers going into battle, their future uncertain. He responded as he would in that situation, with confidence. "You're not going to die. We'll fight it, together, all of us."

Kai broke into a fit of coughing, gasping for breath by the time he was done. The medical staff were all busy working in the lab, so Temms dragged his chair closer to Kai's bed.

"Hey. Come on, now." He took Kai's hand, gripping it hard to get the navigator's attention. "Breathe, slowly, Kai. In, out. Come on." He stared into Kai's panicked eyes, still holding tight. With a shudder, Kai stared back, the focus seeming to help him overcome the compulsion to cough. His breath gradually came under control.

"They're verifying whether you have the disease Lani suspects," the captain explained, keeping a smile on his face to encourage the young man. "If you do, they have a recipe to make the remedy. You'll be fine."

Kai closed his eyes and lay still for several minutes, his breathing still rough, though better managed. "I'd follow you into the second hell if you asked me," he whispered.

Where did that come from?

Temms leaned closer. "What, Kai?"

"You'll look out for me. You look out for everyone." Kai took a deep unsteady breath, and then shifted on the bed.

Just the vote of confidence I needed.

Temms felt the smile creep onto his lips like a wallflower to the dance floor. "Thanks, Kai. I'll try not to get us into any of the hells. It's my general policy."

Kai gave faint smile and then fell silent again, his face relaxing as time passed. The drugs had apparently kicked in. He was asleep, like the rest of them.

Temms repositioned himself on the hard chair, trying to find a comfortable angle, but it didn't come to him. His comm buzzed, and he got up, stepping away from the sick people before he answered.

"Rogers."

"Captain, you'd better come to the bridge," came Tasiq's R-rolling purr.

He groaned. "What now?"

"Stand by."

Brow furrowed, Temms leaned against the door frame to the back room, waiting. A message finally appeared on his comm: *TO: Capt. Temms Rogers, ship* Doubtful. *Clearly, you have not understood the gravity of the trouble you are in. You have ignored our requests and your open defiance leads others to rebel, which we cannot tolerate. You have one last chance. We will give you five days to provide us with coordinates to the artificial satellite in orbit between Terza and Perpetra. If you fail to comply with this request, your rights to navigate in this area of space will be rescinded. If you are found in Agency-monitored space after that time, your ship will be confiscated pursuant to Section 348B of the Interstellar Agreements, and your crew arrested for trespass.*

The message was signed: Senior Agent Delcin, Agency ship *Shelim.*

Temms read it three times before he could fully assimilate the content. Having failed to kill him along with his man on the surface, the Agency thought it could ban him from space? What nonsense.

Annoyed, but well on the way to furious, he walked to the entrance to the lab area. "Lani, I've got another fire to put out. Do you need anything else to get your task completed?"

She paused only a moment, brushing her blonde hair back from her face with a gloved hand. "Not now. I'll let you know." Her gaze was intent. "I'll get Tommy healed and back at your side, Temms. Don't worry about that."

He nodded. "I expect they'll soon be on their way to recovery, all of them. I'll wish you luck anyway. We all need a little luck."

"Is there anything I can do for you, Temms?"

Her tone seemed more intimate than a doctor inquiring of a potential patient. The look in her eyes spoke of longing. He still hadn't been able to have the quiet time he wanted to speak to her about his long-term thoughts.

Damnation. Doesn't look like there will be any time soon, either.

"Lani, we're both busy people. Let's deal with what's right in front of us, all right? I've got every confidence in you."

The doctor stiffened and stepped back. "Of course, Captain."

"Thank you. Keep me posted." Feeling like a cad, he added a silent prayer for success as he left the infirmary, headed for his office. Luck would be nice, but it wasn't on his horizon at the moment. Long past that. What he needed now were answers. He had to look up this Interstellar Agreement and check the section, just to make sure he wasn't being conned in some way. Then he intended to call in some favors.

No one was going to tell him where he could fly. No one.

CHAPTER 15

PRINCE Arlen granted Temms' request to visit security-locked Perpetra for a discussion about the Agency, but the concession didn't come without strings.

"Your Bellonans are not welcome to land here with you." In the monitor's view, Arlen's jaw set like concrete. "When they left my employ, and their herd, they knew they could not return."

"I understand," Temms replied, thinking it was an odd demand for Arlen to throw down, considering Temms hadn't even suggested that Tabio or Aronka accompany him.

The two had made the hard decision to avoid being paired off with others of their kind at the close of their contract term with the Prince. They had left Perpetra with the *Doubtful*, now fully committed to each other. They had a son, Rey, and another child on the way.

But they were alone.

Though the ship had visited Arlen's estate several times since then, the Bellonans had never asked to disembark. Arlen had never addressed it, either.

So something new must be on the horizon. Trouble with the herd? We all have troubles.

"Thank you for agreeing to see me," he said. "We'll be there in about twelve hours."

"Safe travels, Captain." The screen went black.

Travel to Perpetra ate nearly a quarter of the time the Agency had allotted to produce the information on the Ancients' station, but this was something better discussed face to face. He had to assume that any communications he sent would be monitored by the Agency, or its spies. This could be true, even considering that the Cartesian Consortium, to which Prince Arlen belonged, was a high-tech, security-savvy organization. Temms reflected that his last dealings with the Consortium seemed to stop just short of a total strip search before his team was allowed on the planet.

But the Agency had its own shadowy secrets, and he didn't want to take the risk.

He left his office and went up the hall to the bridge. His survey from the top of the rectangular deck felt empty, even though all the seats were filled. It felt wrong to him without Kai, without Liang, without Tommy.

"Captain on deck," Nim said, vacating the captain's seat along the rear wall. Those working paused to straighten up, giving the captain a little nod or recognition. It wasn't a military ship. No salute was necessary.

"Carry on," Temms murmured, coming down to take his seat.

"How's the chief?" Nim asked quietly.

Temms forced a smile. "I think he'll be all right. Thanks for asking."

Nim nodded and moved to the bridge security station.

Temms checked his monitor. As he expected, Liang had left him a message.

Pathogen isolated. The doctor was correct. Developing serum now. No changes expected for at least thirty-six hours. Back on the bridge soon.

A muttered curse escaped him. He likely wouldn't have any of his experienced officers back before the Agency's deadline passed. If it came down to a battle, he wanted his best people in these chairs. His position was unacceptable, but he didn't have any control over the situation. All he could do now was pray the serum worked and he would lose no more of his crew to this mysterious illness.

He sent Liang an acknowledgment, and then let go of the medical situation the best he could. Micromanaging Okalani's department wouldn't get him any farther ahead. He needed to puzzle out the best way to handle the coming confrontation.

He took a deep breath, putting his faculties together. His crew worked at their stations, talking quietly among themselves, even smiling at shared conversation. The sounds of the machinery, its whirrs and beeps, underlay his perception, serving to place him in familiar territory. This was his ship, his home, his family. Given time, he was confident he could come up with the answers he needed to save them all.

Delcin had definitely upped the stakes in the game he played. The Agency wanted this station, if it existed, badly enough to extort the information any way possible. Why this particular tactic? Temms hadn't heard of anyone actually being arrested by the Agency. The usual approach was to hire mercenaries to terrorize the information from people, as they had seen with the holo of Jak Moster.

Granted, Temms tended to be careful and didn't set up himself or his officers to be captured. But "arrest" was a different animal. That involved specific charges of criminal activity, and implied some sort of trial and incarceration. Was that really possible? Where did they keep their prisoners, on one of their ships or on a planetary facility somewhere? And how long could they be jailed? So many of them had no ties to anyone here, would someone come looking for them if they simply disappeared?

What good would it serve to lock us up until we provided information in this case? We don't have any more than rumor of this accursed station. That and my crazy dreams.

Maybe next time the Ancients came calling in his sleep, he could ask them for defenses against the Agency. They had certainly helped him out with the threat of Burko.

If wishes were horses.

What else did he have that was concrete?

He found it hard to trust his own mind, cluttered with worries over his son and the others down in the infirmary, still struggling with the inconceivable loss of Hal, pressured on all sides. Brainstorming with a group would help, but his own trusted inner circle was not available.

He had to reach out to his other alliances.

On his order, Tasiq hailed C. T. Dutton, and they made arrangements to rendezvous in space on the way to Perpetra to carve as little time as possible out of their Agency-allotted deadline.

* * *

WHEN the *Doubtful* approached the assigned coordinates, long-range scans showed that three ships awaited them.

His first thought was that the Agency had intercepted the message and intended to stop the discussion, but none of them seemed at first scan to be an Agency ship. C. T.'s rectangular, squat cargo ship *Fuego* hung in space, flanked by a sleek and silvery ship that looked like an undersea glider fish, and a rust-colored, full-bellied cargo ship Temms thought was Garrett Rawls' *Six-Shooter.*

Now what's going on?

Liang came onto the bridge, hesitating in mid-step as she caught a glance at the common monitor screen. Her face was drawn, dark shadows under her eyes. With a raised eyebrow and curious glance to the captain, she relieved the woman in the navigator's chair. She swiveled in her chair, her gaze moving across those on the bridge as if counting them or looking for someone. She stopped when she got to Nim Williams, her attention lingering there a moment before she turned back to the captain.

"The doctor said to tell you she's making progress. The medicine has been manufactured in sufficient amount."

"Thank you," he said, his fuzzy brain still sorting out what he had just seen. Liang and Nim? Was there something more than professional there? The stray thought that any such match would be more appropriate than one with Jowalt Edwards flitted through, and then vanished. No time for that now.

Tasiq broke into his contemplation. "Captain Dutton suggests you join him on his ship. The others are already there."

"I.D. on the *others?*"

The officer at tactical scanned. "The nav sats identify them as the *Prosperity*, registry Terza, and the *Six-Shooter*, registry unknown."

So he had been right on the one, and the other, the *Prosperity*, belonged to the "twins," Lin Hocai and Xi Pinsan. They had experience and intel on the Agency. The group sounded like just the cross-section of talent to provide him with a wide range of options.

"I guess we'd better take Captain Dutton's suggestion then."

Temms stood up, fumbling for the short list of companions he would want to come along. Two sets of ears analyzing the details were better than his one. Normally, Liang would be the best candidate, but she looked exhausted. Shrugging on the light jacket he left hanging on the back of his chair, he tucked his comm device into his pocket.

"Liang, when's the last time you slept?"

The others on the bridge turned to look at her. She squirmed under their scrutiny.

"Perhaps two days ago." She glanced at Rogers, and then back to the dials and buttons of her station. "I can continue without sleep now, Captain. Particularly if you're going to leave the ship."

"I'm sure you can, but I choose to have everyone keep their immune systems at full health. You're relieved until you get at least four hours' sleep. Preferably eight. If what you've said is true, everyone will be on the mend for the rest of the day. When they start getting functional again, the doctor may need further assistance. In the meantime, we're not going anywhere particular."

She stood but didn't leave her station. "Captain, I—"

"Now, Liang. Please. Get some rest."

Looking defeated, she followed his order and left the bridge.

Who did that leave? Tas would be a good listener. His eye fell on Nim, who looked as excited as a puppy at the prospect of an outing.

Well, why not? If Liang trusted him enough to let him near her carefully-locked heart, I should be able to do the same.

"Nim, come with me. Tas, you've got the bridge."

"Yes, sir!" they said in chorus.

He stopped by his office to pick up a bottle of a rare *bosli*-derived liquor he had been carting around for some time to give to Dutton when next they met. Temms didn't drink the stuff himself—too much fire, not enough warmth. But it was one of Dutton's favorites.

Might as well give it to him now, before we disappear into one of the Agency's forgotten cells.

With that happy thought in mind, he and Nim proceeded down to the lower hatch.

CHAPTER 16

TEMMS helped Nim and Iov to prepare the inflatable airlock, planning to extend it to the *Fuego*. This was a new technological addition he had acquired from this universe, about half a year before, and it saved a good deal of wear and tear on the slipcrafts and other small ships the *Doubtful* carried, at least for short distances.

The cylindrical shell would be inflated until it was hard, which fully extended the longerons inside, and provided support for the meteoroid shield and the other three layers that kept the person inside from cold space. One end attached to the ship, and the other could be used as an exit for an EVA activity, or, as now, attached to another ship that was floating still in space. The entire apparatus was much lighter than the original metal ones that came standard on Confederation ships, and saved space and fuel.

The thought of traversing that eight to twenty meters with no more around him than a fortified plastic bag made him a little nervous. Who wouldn't feel the same way?

"Captain." Nim gave him a tight nod of his dark-haired head then looked behind the captain. "I—I wanted to thank you for choosing me to accompany you."

Temms smiled. The security man had chafed for months behind Tommy's placement as chief of the department. There was no reason to doubt his competence. That's why he had been hired from Sol Aeris. But Temms found it more natural to work with his son.

Transparent though Williams' motives might be, it was time for him to gain some experience.

I can't get caught again at loose ends if my key people are down.

"I'm sure you'll do fine, Nim. Let's break out two breathing masks."

"Yes, sir!"

Williams disappeared into the equipment alcove and the captain chuckled, catching Iov's eye. "Kids," he said.

Iov nodded. "Always I am telling Uri he must hold back. It is not yet his time."

The Muuvos had been abroad for several months now, and Temms had heard no bad reports about them. Hardworking, yes, and willing to fill in as necessary. Nev played a mean stringed instrument, and often led jam sessions in the common room on off hours. But the captain hadn't had time to follow up on a more personal level.

I've got to work on that.

"I hear you're all three strong assets to our little family. You've got everything you need?" he asked. "Quinn's treating you decently?"

Iov shrugged. "Dani is the better leader. But since Halian is gone, Quinn has been most understanding."

"I would agree with that. I'm sorry I haven't checked in more often. Your adjustment is important to me. But with so much going on—"

Iov shook his head. "Crisis is crisis. No need for explanation, or apology. We know where is your office. If we have problem, we can find the doorstep."

"Agreed."

Williams returned with two breathing apparatuses. Each had a mask that covered the full face and made a tight seal, attached by a rubber tube to a small container of oxygen that hooked on the belt. They weren't intended to save a life in open space—in those circumstances, a full EVA suit would be worn—but simply to assure that if some small leak occurred in a crossing, that the traveler would have air to breathe until he or she reached the other side.

The thick mask must have been put away with condensation still in it, because the surface oozed a faint moldy smell that was off-putting. He wiped it out with an antibac cloth, and then fastened it onto his face. He picked up the bag that held his notepads and the precious bottle and looped it over his shoulder. Once Temms and Williams had checked their seal, Iov signaled that they were ready to leave the ship.

"Send the tube out," Temms said.

Iov complied, and Temms and Williams watched as the shell extended in the direction of Dutton's ship. The seconds passed, seeming to pass ever more slowly.

"Full extension," Iov finally said.

Shortly afterward, Tasiq's voice came over the intercom. "The *Fuego* is ready to receive you, captain. The airlock is sealed onto his hatch, and instruments indicate it is fully pressurized."

"Thank you, Tas." Rogers rolled his shoulders, ready to get the transit over with. "Nim?"

The security man was already in the opening gate to the lock, practically bursting to prove himself. "Ready when you are, sir."

"Let's do it."

Temms took a step into the airlock on the *Doubtful*, waiting until Iov sealed the hatch behind him and Williams before reaching for the seal to the suspended tube that led over to the other ship.

All I have to do is step out there onto that plastic floor.

He fought the impulse to stare at that floor. Though he knew from the many times he had used the tube it was sturdy enough to carry him, his imagination always led him to a vision of placing his foot down to find it went right through. The hole he created would rip open from the pressure and he would be sucked out into space, never to return.

"Captain?" Williams bumped his shoulder. "Everything all right?"

Temms cleared his throat. "Just making sure." He dragged his eyes up to stare at the hatch at the far end of the tube, and focused there instead. Such a blessing that the plastic walls of the tube were opaque so the stars weren't visible. Just like a regular corridor in the ship. Any ship. Just march.

One step in front of the other.

"I'll go first. It's my job," Williams said, and he gently pushed past the captain, pulling himself along by the handholds on the side of the tube that kept those crossing upright. He crossed in what seemed to be a few breaths, his feet barely brushing the floor, and then paused outside the hatch of the *Fuego*.

Temms took a deep breath and hauled himself across, watching Williams the whole time, trying to ignore the fact he was vulnerable in space. Any piece of debris moving fast enough could just come along and—*Stop!*

The sudden grip of anxiety over this showed how much stress he had loaded onto his shoulders. He had used this tube a hundred times. While he had never been perfectly comfortable, in his logical mind, he knew the efficiency and low cost of using it made sense. The thing telescoped to nearly twenty meters, but Dutton's ship seemed closer than that. With both ships in hover mode, they would be just fine.

All the same, he felt so much better once they entered the safe, closed hatch of the *Fuego*.

C. T. met them at the hatch, grinning.

"What's all the mystery, friend?" Temms asked as Dutton clasped his hand in greeting.

"You'll see."

C. T. led Temms and Williams down a corridor into the heart of the ship. The farther they went, Temms detected the aroma of fried spices, onions and garlic. His stomach rumbled. How long had it been since he stopped to eat? *Probably as long as Liang had pushed herself without sleep.*

The thought that he and his crew were equally strung out brought him a chuckle, and he was in a more relaxed frame of mind as he entered the *Fuego's* dining room, its round table set with plates and bowls of steaming food.

Garrett Rawls sat at the far end of the table, leather booted feet propped up on an end table off to the left. "Since everyone was coming, Valeni and Nikki insisted on fixing y'all a mess of vittles."

Temms dug in his bag for the bottle and handed it to C. T., whose eyes widened a moment before his big smile. "Forgot this when we were at Roandock."

"No problem," the other captain said. "I'll enjoy it just the same." He tucked it away in a cupboard, and gestured to the table.

"I don't have time for this," Temms muttered, to the sincere regret of his stomach.

"You don't have time not to hear this," C. T. scolded. "Sit, eat, and listen."

Williams hesitated at Temms' shoulder, but it didn't take an empath to sense his hunger for the sustenance set before them, as well as for the pretty girls. They latched onto him immediately, finding him a chair and handing him a serving spoon.

Temms sighed. "No more than thirty minutes."

"Deal."

C. T. took a seat at the other end of the table. The two young women fluttered about until they were joined by Hocai and Pinsan, who wore matching black slacks and red silk embroidered jackets with high collars. They bowed to Temms, and then took seats as Valeni directed. Once they were seated, Nikki finished putting bowls on the table, and they set to their meal.

The food was excellent, certainly a gift to his stressed system. His mind still ensnared in the Agency's deadline, Temms followed the meal with some hot Lapsang tea, watching the faces around the table. Everyone seemed to know something they were anxious to share.

"So what is it? Something must be about to set the heavens ablaze to make you haul me off this track."

Hocai leaned forward, her black hair in long braids that hung in front of her shoulders. "The Agency has given you an ultimatum, yes?"

Temms' eyes narrowed. "How do you know that? Has Delcin done the same to others?"

"No," she replied in concert with the others. "What are the terms?"

"I've got little over three days to come up with some information. They've threatened to ban me from Marriel-Terzan airspace if I can't give them what they want. Or arrest us."

Valeni gasped, and Nikki put an arm around her.

Temms shrugged. "Frankly, I'm not sure they can even do that."

"They can." C. T.'s expression was solemn. "It wouldn't be the first time they've done that to a ship and a captain."

"What are they going to do? Blow me out of the sky?"

"The last man they warned was Lassa Bitman. Now granted, he had no respect for the Agency's orders at all. Didn't pay the excises demanded, either. But word got around he had a mark on him, and shortly after, he and his ship disappeared." C. T. stirred his kaffe thoughtfully. "Saw the ship again, but it had been sold, new markings and all. And it sure wasn't Lassa at the helm."

Temms frowned and eyed Hocai. "How did you know I'd received an ultimatum?"

She looked at Pinsan. "We still have our connections."

"You mean you're spying for them?" Nim broke in, dropping his fork onto his plate with a clatter.

Pinsan jumped to his feet. "How dare you—"

"Whoa, hold on," Garrett said, now sitting straight and gaze fully alert, even a little sharp. "No one's accusing anyone of claptrap like that, not here. We're all friends, here to help each other."

Temms gestured to Nim. "Enough. We came to hear what they had to say, and we'll hear it."

All the same, Nim's accusation reminded him that the *twins* had been allied with the Agency, once upon a time, and that tended to make him a little paranoid about sharing information. If they had discovered his conversation with the Agency through their channels, perhaps he shouldn't tell them anything else.

Even if he truly believed they were on his side.

"What is it they want, Temms?" C. T. asked.

Temms sipped his smoky tea, deciding what was safe to reveal. "You know they're interested in this mythical station. Probably think there's all sort of technology in there they can steal."

"You're not taking them to it, are you?" Pinsan demanded. "You can't do that!"

Pinsan's tone proved his belief that the station was real. That made Temms even more curious. How many people had gotten these enigmatic messages about the station and its missing parts? If the

Ancients wanted Temms' help, why hadn't they been more forthcoming with details where to find the blasted thing?

Frustration seized his throat and choked him. Coughing, he set his cup down. "I'm not taking them there. I don't even know where it is. Or if it's real."

"It's real," Hocai said. "It's real."

"Have you been there?" Nim asked, skepticism underlining his voice.

She looked away and didn't answer.

Aha, there's more suspicion here than just mine. Somehow that reassured Temms a great deal.

"You think the Consortium has answers for you?" C. T. asked.

He had hardly opened his mouth to answer when Hocai interrupted. "You can't think to involve the Consortium. They're every bit as bad as the Agency."

"Hardly," Temms said. "The Consortium is perfectly happy to mind its own business and not tell me how to run mine."

Nikki got up from the table and started clearing away dishes. Valeni joined her, but her attention was clearly split between the domestic tasks and the conversation.

"But you don't understand," Hocai persisted. "The Ancients have no wish to support the way the Agency does business, but neither do they favor the Cartesian Consortium. If the station is properly activated, the power contained there will realign business across the entire star system. Everything will change. Everything."

Temms considered his dreams and the messages he had received. True that no promises had been made in support of any particular scheme, other than to help "all" their progeny. They had been vague about exactly how or who would benefit.

"Don't you see? If you reveal this base to either the Agency or the Consortium, then the station's under a real threat. The Agency has sniffed around, looking for it, but so far they haven't got the resources to actually locate it."

Her dark eyes flashed as she looked around the table at them. "The Consortium has superior investigative tools. We've been fortunate that they haven't taken an interest to date. They could hunt it down and destroy it before the facility can be used for good."

"What's your interest, ma'am?" Garrett asked. "Sounds to me like you're wanting to control it just as much as any of the rest of these old boys."

Pinsan laid his hand on his sister's arm, and she sat back in her seat, falling silent. The sounds of the dishes being washed up, soft splash of water, clank of silverware, these things seemed to swallow up the air.

Finally Pinsan spoke. "Our Elders have long taught respect for the work of the Ancients, those who built civilizations long ago and laid the paths for us to follow. For many years they seemed lost to us. Only in the last year have there been signs of their return."

He looked directly at Temms. "Your search for and use of the Ancients' artifacts has become known to us. Whether you have awakened the Ancients, or whether they have used your strength to make themselves known once again, it is apparent that their return to power is imminent."

"Is that a good thing?" Nim asked. "I mean, how do we know they aren't even worse than either the Consortium or the Agency? Who wants to set up a sector-wide dictatorship?"

"They're not like that," Temms said. "I don't know how to explain it, but when we were in contact with them, I could sense only benevolence. They mean well."

Hocin beamed. "Yes. Exactly."

Seeing Nim was ready to argue the point, Temms cut him off. "The Agency learned about our use of the artifacts from Burko, without my knowledge. I hadn't really considered any impact of the station on any other entity but the Agency. Whatever I could use to get them off my back, I'm willing to try it. But we don't really know that activating the station could upset the balance of power. Could the Agency crumble? Or the Consortium? No way of knowing."

C. T. finished his ale. "Certainly not enough solid information available for my comfort, either way."

Disappointment filled Temms' heart. He certainly hoped to persuade Prince Arlen to assist him against the Agency, but he also wanted to access Consortium records about the potential of a station of the Ancients' near their orbit. Perhaps it wasn't a dead issue. He would play that one by ear. If they brought up the subject of Rogers' current artifact collection and his interest in acquiring more, then he might feel out their level of interest.

The party started to break up. Pinsan and C. T. finished clearing the table, while Nim went for the head. Temms' gaze slowly came back around to Garrett Rawls, who had returned to his laid-back, propped-up position. When their eyes met, Garrett reached up and tapped the brim of his hat.

"Everyone's got advice, don't they? So many cards in play, it's hard to keep them counted."

Temms mulled over several possible interpretations of Garrett's words. Counting cards? As in keeping track of what's been dealt? Or guessing what new combinations would be laid out? He judged the expression on Garrett's broad face, the sparkle of amusement in his green eyes. "I suppose that means you have some advice, too?"

Garrett sat forward and shrugged. "All this is only as good as what it means to you, Captain. Man's got to ride his own path through the desert."

"Ah, right."

"The gals, now, they've kept their ears open ever since they heard you were searching out more artifacts. Word on the waves is that you're the man, the expert in these things. If the Agency's on the trail of such materials, you can bet they're going to be right after you. If you're going hell-bent for this station, they're going to dog you all the way there."

Temms conceded that point. "So I'll be careful."

Garrett grinned and drained his dark ale. "Like I said, 'sup to you. From what I hear, you got no troubles taking care of yourself."

"No troubles?" Temms laughed and glanced over to C. T. "Well, I appreciate a good wingman, now and then. Like I tell Tom all the time, I'll always listen to what people have to say. I may not follow that advice, but I'll take responsibility for that."

He checked the time again. "I really need to be on my way, friends. You've given me a lot to think about. Thanks for the meal, ladies. It was amazing."

Nikki and Valeni came over to him, each warmly embracing him and Nim before they could get away. "We're happy you enjoyed it, Captain."

C. T. walked them down to the hatch, hands in his pockets. "Keep us posted," he said.

"You'll be the first to know."

They left the hatch, negotiating the waiting connector tube. Nim was several steps ahead of him, Iov verifying the integrity of the structure before his captain entered it.

Temms felt like he was in a good place. He had a good team, and good friends who cared about how he was doing. In the next few days, he would have the rest of his staff upright again, and all would be well in the universe. If he could just get through the next couple of days.

CHAPTER 17

OKALANI'S relief grew over the next hours that passed, as the treatment gleaned from the old records began to have visible effects on her overcrowded infirmary.

Those most recently affected reacted almost immediately. Kai was awake and eating on his own in less than a day. Dani and Riviera took nearly four days to come completely off the ventilators and begin interacting again. Lavan scarcely left Dani's side, even staying with her during his off-duty hours, jumping to get anything she needed.

Tommy Rogers took a couple of days to shake off the effects of the infection, but his attitude, so like his father's, seemed to force him through. Before his confinement, Okalani hadn't had a lot of contact with the young man, as he tended to hang with a different social crowd, and their schedules and duties kept them in different places. She found his optimism and drive as he cheered on the recovery of the others endeared him to her and the rest of the medical staff.

Exhausted from weeks of inhumanly long days on duty, she couldn't let herself take too long away, not until every one of those beds were empty again. But entering reports into the computer system proved less than stimulating. Her heavy eyelids kept closing even while she sat at her desk, struggling to finish.

"Hey, Doc, why don't you just call it a day?"

The voice came from the chair beside her, startling her enough that she snapped awake. Tommy's blue eyes studied her, his head cocked, and he tapped the desk near her hand with his index finger.

Guilt flashed through her. "Oh! I'm sorry, hon. Did you need something?"

She glanced around the infirmary, wondering how Tommy had snuck up on her. Nev stood next to Riviera's bed, steadying her as she sat on the edge of the mattress, working her legs to rebuild the strength in them. Lavan fed Dani something out of a crockery bowl.

If he'd had an emergency, there's no reason why Tom couldn't have asked one of them for something. No, he was definitely focused on her.

"I'm good," he said. "I'm more worried about you at this point. You've been at this pretty much non-stop for days. It says a lot for your dedication, but where will we be if you work yourself into your own sickbed, hmm?" He waved a finger at her in a scolding manner. "More importantly, where will my dad be?"

Where had that come from? Had she missed something? She had definitely gotten the impression Temms wasn't going to pursue any permanent relationship with her. It did hurt her feelings, but she was a grown woman. She understood. So why would Tommy say this about his father? Her earlier guilt changed to panic. "Is your father ill?"

"What? No." Surprise on his face turned to understanding. "I didn't mean that. I meant, you know. Him. You." He gestured with his hands, bringing his index fingers side by side. "The two of you."

"Oh." Her eyes suddenly burned. She tried to blink away the tears before they dripped rudely down her face.

His jaw went slack. "Hey, hey, now." He took her hands, pulled his chair closer. "I didn't mean anything horrible by that. I'm so sorry. I just wanted to be encouraging. You've done such a great job, and I know he knows that."

How could she explain that the captain's attitude over the last few weeks had made it very clear to her that she wasn't one of his priorities? She had come near to breaking many times during the crisis, and he hadn't been able to take time for her once. Not once.

"He's not interested, Tom. He's made it clear. It's all right. He has so many people counting on him. I can't expect him to—" The blunt admission of her failure to another living person, and the release of pressure now that everyone seemed to be recovering tore down her reserves, and the tears kept coming. In seconds, she was sobbing, her hands covering her face.

"By the gods, I didn't mean to hurt you!"

Before she realized what was happening, Tommy had pulled his chair right in front of hers and had his arms around her, her head on his shoulder. His right hand patted her back so gently, she couldn't even move. She needed what he was providing—a little support and comfort.

And it was only fair, right, after I spent so many hours trying to save all of them? Him, too? I can just let him be nice to me.

But the longer they sat so close, despite her deluge, she became aware of his muscular arms and chest, the male smell of him, strong after several days of fever. What was she doing?

Her hands still holding him tight, some corner of her brain that still clung to rationality calculated up his age—what was he, twenty-two? Twenty-three? Temms was on the far side of fifty.

And you're not even thirty yet. So whose ball park does that put you in, missy?
It could happen.

Startled at the realization, she pulled away from Tommy, using her reach for a handful of face wipes as an excuse to let go.

"You should be in bed," she sniffed.

"Can't keep a good man down." His grin reminded her of his father's. They had the same charm. Why had she never noticed until now?

"Well, that's where you're wrong, my friend." She stood and took his arm, leading him back to bed. "You're not ready for action yet."

"Action?" His grin faded and then returned, a very different look in his eyes. "I wasn't looking for action. Just yet." He winked.

A little surprised at herself, she looked around and caught Lavan's eyes on her. His gaze wasn't quite disapproving, but definitely seemed to question what she was doing. She had to get away and think about it. Tommy was her patient. A very sick patient, finally starting to get well again. She needed to let him recover and get back to work.

What happened then would be anyone's guess.

She cleared her throat and stepped back. "Maybe you're right. I've been on duty much too long. You're all getting ready to leave me in the next day or so, and I'll have my quiet space back." She wiped her face again. "Please forgive my unprofessional behavior. Things happen when we're under stress."

"Get some sleep," he said gently. "You'll feel better. Don't worry, things will work out."

He reached for her hand, but she was too far away.

"Good night, then." She turned to Lavan. "If you need me, I'll be in my quarters."

"Yes, ma'am." Lavan studied her, and then turned back to Dani, who managed a weak wave to the doctor.

Okalani retreated to her quarters, taking time for a long, super-hot shower to wash all the infirmary germs and smells from her. She nearly sent Temms a message, out of habit, but something kept her from it. Instead, she put on one of her long, white nightgowns she had brought with her for her wedding trousseau and slid between fresh sheets. As exhausted as she was, she expected to fall right to sleep, but she didn't.

Instead she found herself replaying in her head the mental pictures of the slow awakenings the staff under her care had made, Dani whimpering as she finally opened her eyes, Riviera stoic as always, but finally gifting them all with her broad smile. She had managed to save them, and it was a great blessing.

What stuck with her most, however, was the feel of Tommy Rogers' arms around her, and how much she enjoyed it. Guilt and a sense of betrayal washed over her, but all the same, it's not like the captain hadn't had his chance. She had practically thrown herself at him. And he had turned her down.

Guess we'll just have to take this decision one day at a time.

In the meantime, she cherished the reminder that she was a pretty woman who might well be wanted by a man. It was a pleasant jumping off place for a night of lighter dreams.

CHAPTER 18

COMPARED to the past few weeks, the trip to Perpetra was uneventful.

His bridge officers were back to duty. Liang was back to only working one shift per day. Kai, looking a lot more flushed and healthy than he had just days before, monitored the voyage and reported two Agency ships at different times scanning the *Doubtful*. But they never contacted the ship or interfered with their travel.

It didn't mean that Temms could put their surveillance out of his mind. His fascination with the potential of a station left by the Ancients after all the effects they had already had on his life was unavoidable. They practically invited him to come.

Why him?

Why not someone from the Agency, or from the Consortium?

He had only been in this place for a year. They had been here all along. Why hadn't the Ancients revealed themselves to those who had been here before him?

He had no answer.

Certainly he had crossed the boundaries between universes, using the Ancient's tech, which set him apart from the locals, but he wasn't the only one to do that. Garrett Rawls, if his tale was true, had come from a different place as well. But he had never mentioned the Ancients, nor did he seem to understand the use of the Ancients' technology. So that couldn't be it.

"Entering Consortium space, Captain." Kai reported, interrupting Temms' musings.

He straightened in his chair, rolling his shoulders to relieve tension. "Prepare to present our identification."

Prince Arlen's scanned package of diplomatic paperwork cleared the way for the ship to penetrate the buoyed boundaries of the Cartesian Consortium. He had visited the blue-bauble world of Perpetra on several occasions over the year, sometimes at the behest of the Prince and other times on the business of the Consortium's head office on Terza. It wasn't the sort of place one went without a strict invitation.

When he reported to the chilly slipcraft bay, he found Tabio waiting for him, in human form. Emotion flushed his normally olive skin. He spoke quickly, as if he expected the captain to cut him off before he could finish.

"Captain, we would like to request the opportunity to attend you at Perpetra. It has been more than a year, and even though—"

Much as he hated to damp Tabio's enthusiasm, he had no choice. "You can't."

The Bellonan stiffened, pain crossing his face like he had been slapped.

Temms rubbed a hand over his eyes. "I'd like nothing better than to take you back with me. The Prince specifically requested that you not come to the planet. I take it he's not a man who forgets his orders."

Tabio's shoulders fell. "I understand, sir. I will tell Aronka."

"For what it's worth, I don't agree with him. But I'm under a deadline here and I need to get our situation straightened out first. The time will come to address this issue, I promise you."

Tabio nodded, and then turned on his heel and walked out. Temms wasn't sure which of them felt worse about the interchange.

Liang and Nim walked into the bay, talking quietly. They stopped when they noticed him, and he thought they moved apart. *Or maybe that's just my paranoia and nerves talking.* He had been too busy to investigate his theory that there was something going on between his first officer and security man.

"Captain," Nim said, with a formal nod.

Liang glanced back over her shoulder. "Tabio seemed distressed."

Temms nodded. "I had to tell him the Prince forbid their visit."

"I wondered why you'd selected me for this trip," Nim said. "I knew the Chief wasn't quite up to the effort just yet. So I guess I'm next on the chain."

Liang frowned at Nim, and then turned back to the captain. "The prince seemed very clear on his conditions for their leaving his service. A misunderstanding wouldn't seem possible."

Temms shook his head, picking up his case. "I'd thought so. They've seemed happy enough here."

Liang crossed her arms, shifting her weight onto her left leg. "Perhaps they are only now realizing the long-term consequences of their choice. At the time, their primary consideration was their love, but with a child, and another on the way, they must be concerned about the future prospects for those offspring, cut off from the rest of their kind."

"People do crazy things for love," Nim said, with a knowing smile for Liang.

Well, that proves it.

Not quite sure he was ready to lose his "daughter" yet, Temms cleared his throat. "I've got other agenda items with a higher priority. Come on. Our entry window will be a brief one."

Liang piloted the slipcraft to the designated coordinates near the palace. They landed without fanfare, where a half dozen black-uniformed minions of the Prince waited to take them inside the palace.

They were escorted through a side door into an anteroom lined with heavy red velvet curtains from ceiling to floor, and then on into a large conference room with a rectangular table some twelve feet across. The two side walls consisted of polished wood bookcases holding stacks upon stacks of leather-covered volumes. The third wall was a huge picture window that revealed the inner gardens of the palace. Temms caught a glimpse of a hedge maze and a collection of brilliantly-flowered roses before they were marched past the table, left to stand, waiting, on the thick carpet in a sophisticated geometric design of cream and midnight blue.

The minions took up positions at the several doorways to the room. Two young girls in black uniforms quickly entered and set trays on the table's polished mahogany surface, one tray with small, delicately-cut sandwiches, the other with a chilled pitcher of water and several glasses. Then the servants vanished.

As the minutes passed, and they remained alone with the guards, Temms allowed a fleeting worry that something had changed. Perhaps the prince had decided against sharing information with them, or that the Agency's pursuit had gotten too close.

Or perhaps he just enjoyed making a grand entrance.

Liang and Nim, both familiar with the exacting security, said nothing, but remained standing straight, next to their captain. Temms gave Liang a wink, and then waited as patiently as he could. He still had two days before the Agency's ultimatum deadline, but he didn't want to wait until the last minute to test their resolve.

Suddenly the Prince swept into the room with several more sycophants in tow, his silver hair immaculately combed, his formal jacket in a dark plum, his boots polished to a slick shine. The arrival was so dramatic, Temms was surprised it wasn't accompanied by a trumpet fanfare.

Definitely the grand entrance type.

The tall man stood across the table from the *Doubtful* team, his patrician face lit with a gentle smile. "Captain Rogers, welcome to our home."

"Your Highness." Temms inclined his head, short of an actual bow.

The Prince gestured to Temms' companions. "Officer Chen, Officer Williams, please have a seat."

The Prince has done his homework. Or at least one of his lackeys did.

Temms allowed a slight smile as he held one of the chairs for Liang, and then took the one next to her. Williams took the one on the far side of Liang. The Prince and two of his aides sat across from them. One of the underlings passed napkins and the trays and they all helped themselves to something to drink and eat, setting their choices on woven mats.

When they had been served, the Prince started eating, applying himself to the thin sandwiches with gusto. He hardly looked up. Temms recognized the tactic for what it was—another indication of who had control.

Guess he knows I'm here with my hat in my hand. This time.

He resolved to exact a sweet revenge the next time Arlen needed something from him instead.

He and his team ate enough to be polite, but finished before the Prince, so they were ready to talk. Arlen finally wiped his hands on a large cloth napkin, and then leaned forward, his elbows on the table. "So, Captain, what is it you need from me?"

Temms had considered half a dozen lines to open with, unsure how the conversation would go. Since Arlen had laid it right on the table, he would do the same.

"A group of captains has banded together to challenge the Agency's tariff structure. Their demands have gotten more and more outrageous, and we need to set some limits, or we're not going to be able to continue to do business."

One of the aides whispered in Arlen's ear. The Prince nodded and looked thoughtful.

"It's more than just financial pressure. The Agency won't get its own hands dirty, of course, but they hire mercenaries to carry out deadly retribution against captains and ships they find uncooperative."

He set a datapad on the table, activating the holo of Jak Moster's murder. The Prince watched, stony-faced, though some of his men looked away.

"They've attacked and killed one of my people on Roandock as well. An Agent named Delcin has put the target square on my ship, and I have every reason to believe he means it. I need some help."

Arlen pursed his lips, and then took a long drink from his glass. "What did you do?"

From the corner of his eye, Temms saw Nim stiffen, his hand clenched around his glass. Liang sat still as a breath, her face impassive.

She'd be one hell of a card player. I've got to get her into the game one of these days.

"I expressed my opposition to their tariffs." Temms shrugged. "Fairly vehemently."

Arlen nodded, but didn't speak.

"There may also be a certain organizing of other captains. Strength in numbers, you know the kind of thing. Looking to change Agency policy, if it's possible."

He paused there, thinking he had explained enough to test Arlen's willingness to become involved. After his talk with Hocin, he wanted to be cautious with the issue of the missing station. *Last resort, only.*

After a long silence, the prince leaned back in his chair, steepling his fingers in front of him. "As you know, Captain, our long-standing arrangements with the Agency entail agreements to co-exist without interference from the other. We control the rights around Perpetra and also the interplanetary space between Perpetra and Terzan's eastern hemisphere. The Consortium conducts its business without any tariffs from the Agency. They also stay out of our designated space." He took a measured drink of his icy water. "Realistically, your group can't negotiate such an understanding."

"Agreed."

"What efforts have you made to broker a solid pact with them?"

Temms laid out the various tactics the captains had proposed, and the failure of each. "They're not interested in negotiating. It's take it or leave it."

Arlen nodded and leaned back in his chair. He studied those with Temms, and then turned his attention on the Captain. "And *leave it* leaves you unable to conduct business."

"Exactly."

"What do you think I can do for you?"

Now there was the million-credit question.

He put on a confident smile. "You're a man of considerable power and influence. I thought you could—"

"Intervene with the Agency on your behalf?" His voice held deep incredulity. "Captain, I respect your rights as an independent businessman, and I've come to like you personally, as well. But you cannot expect that I would violate every covenant between the Agency and the Cartesian Consortium for the benefit of one man. Even one who's been of service to me."

Temms wrestled with the scowl that threatened to take over his face. Did Arlen really think he would come crawling to ask for help if he had other options? Under the table's edge, his hand curled into a fist. He glanced at his people. Liang was engaged, sitting up straight. Nim had relaxed, sitting back in his seat with a tolerant smile on his face.

"The Agency's going to run down the indie captains first," Temms said. "Then when they think they're big enough, they'll challenge everyone else in the sector. If they get hold of the right technology...." He choked back his words, before he revealed his concerns about the Ancients' station. Feigning a cough, he took a drink of water, letting his thoughts fall into better order.

The prince studied him, curiosity lighting his eyes. "If you have specific information of a threat, Captain Rogers, you should tell me now. You owe me that."

Temms considered dropping the name of Tuon Donn. Would it really make a difference in the face of Arlen's reluctance? He shook his head. "Nothing specific. Just knowing how the Agency works. They'll keep collecting weapons until they find one that can take down any enemy who stands in their way."

"There's something more."

Liang spoke quietly next to him. "Sir, you should tell him."

What in blazes was she doing? Unsure what direction she was headed, he stalled. "I'm not sure he'll understand."

"You've lost crew, nearly lost half a dozen more, your son included." She turned to the prince and his aides. "You must forgive him if he is not thinking as clearly as usual. He's hardly slept while we battled the Eckiner's Syncytium virus aboard the ship."

Temms was gratified to see a flash of fear in the aides' eyes.

"The Eckiner's Syncytium virus? That's been eradicated for years," the prince said.

"Not for those who came with the Captain into this universe. We discovered it very late." She leaned forward in her seat. "Thank the gods that our doctor was able to manufacture the cure, which was out of supply here. We only lost one, Halian. You might remember him, a large, furry alien. He came here with us when we brought your granddaughter home." She glanced at Temms. "He's just too proud to admit he's not invincible."

The prince cocked his head. "Yes, I believe I do remember him." He studied Temms. "I'm sorry for your loss."

Temms cleared his throat, wondering if Arlen really bought that diversion.

Better sell it.

"There's no reason to bother him with our personal tragedies," he snapped at Liang.

Then he turned to the prince. "I can handle what happens on my ship," he informed as seriously as he could make it sound. "I've brought the issue of the Agency to you, because they're a potential problem for all of us."

Arlen stood. "As I said, I'm sorry for your loss. As for the Agency, I'm sorry I can't help you. The Consortium and the Agency are at equilibrium, a state attained only after years of conflict and negotiation. We cannot upset that."

"I'm sorry to hear that." Temms and his team got to their feet. "Thank you for seeing us. My regards to your family."

The prince inclined his head in dismissal, and then he and his men left the room in silence. So different from that splendid entry.

Temms exchanged a knowing glance with Liang, knowing they were probably still monitored. She had diverted the issue of the invisible station. But Arlen's refusal to ally himself with Temms against the Agency threat left him with only one choice.

He would have to pursue the location of this mysterious station himself and enlist the Ancients' help if he were to have any chance to successfully defeat the Agency.

CHAPTER 19

NO matter how he tried to change his fortunes, Temms seemed destined to fail.

First, his spectacularly unfruitful visit with Prince Arlen and the Consortium. Then, convinced only the Ancients could help him now, he had spent the past two nights trying to force contact through his dreams, setting his subconscious to watch before sleep. The only result had been two sleepless nights, and a very cranky attitude.

There has to be something I can do.

Half-drowsing on the bridge, its standard mechanical and electronic noises acting like a lullaby in his deprived state, the captain snapped awake when Tasiq called him.

"Captain?"

He glanced to his right when Tas didn't continue. It was hard to read the expression of the communications officer through his furry brow, but confusion and a hard surprise underlined his voice.

"Private message, sir."

Temms let his gaze slide over the others on the bridge, now back at full complement. The only one who focused on the exchange was Liang.

Of course. She never missed anything.

Temms activated his monitor, plugging in his earpiece so he would have the transmission to himself. What he saw felt like a punch to the gut.

Jak Moster grinned at him from his screen. A deep laugh filtered into Temms' ear. "Didn't expect to see me, I'm sure."

"Can't say I did."

Temms just stared. If Jak had been alive all this time, he had done one hell of a job of good hiding. Where could he be? Aware of Liang's piqued interest, he withheld further comment.

"No one expects to see me, and that's the way I'd like to keep it." Jak rubbed his broad forehead, avoiding a thick red scar that slashed across the right side. His thick chestnut hair, that mane of which he had been so proud, was gone. Jak was bald as a newborn babe.

"I can understand that. You've been keeping busy?"

"You'd better believe it. Trying to keep our Agency friends from getting their hands on a particular artifact."

That raised Temms' eyebrow. "Successfully, to all accounts."

Jak chuckled. "So you're aware of the station? We thought so. But your trail shows you're not aware of its location. You've been visiting with many sources in an attempt to score that bit of information."

Jak's smile faded. "We also know the Agency's put the hurt on you to gain that knowledge."

Where was Jak getting his information? What Temms might reveal really depended on how the data might be used.

"The deadline's about up," Jak added when he didn't respond.

Temms nodded. "True."

"What are you going to tell them, Temms?" Jak's eyes had lost their warmth, and his jaw set with what might be desperation.

"Can't hardly tell them what I don't know."

Temms took a moment to study Jak, letting his perception spread to the area behind the former captain of the *Ramman*. Some sort of conference room, with a large table made out of a flat-toned gray metal, and no windows. The walls were off-white with a copper pattern running along them at a height easily reached by human hands. The pattern was vaguely familiar, but he couldn't place it. He might be on a ship, but intuition told Temms this was not so.

"Even if it puts you out of business?"

"Hmmph. Who says it's going to put me out of business? There's more planets in this star system than Marriel and Terza."

"Be serious. Perpetran space is not a place where you're going to ply your mercenary trade."

Temms didn't bother to reveal that he had already done just that, in assorted secret missions, like the one that had returned a young girl to her grandparents' home in safety. At the same time, he had to concede his conversation with Prince Arlen about his current opportunities had been less than encouraging.

There's Lennor. Don't forget about Lennor.

Right. Home of the disturbed little woman-worshiping priests and the big hairy cave monsters. Not a whole lot of lucrative trade there.

He sighed. "Jak, you know I have no love for the Agency or anything it stands for. The Ancients saved our lives once, and I'd protect them with my own. In fact, they've practically invited me to help them out with this thing. But it's a rhetorical question at best. Bottom line is still that I don't know the location of this place."

Jak seemed to weigh the options and then gave a grin. "Would you like to?"

* * *

A FEW hours later, the *Doubtful* hung in space not too far from the Consortium security-buoyed territorial line in Terza's orbit. Right next to nothing.

Temms had provided the coordinates to Kai Windthorp, and he had followed them to the letter. On arrival, however, Kai turned to the captain, questions in his eyes.

"Captain, I've double-checked the co-ords, but I can't find any sign of a station. Or anything else."

Temms frowned. He had considered the possibility that the setup was a trap, but Jak's offer had seemed genuine. He hadn't shared the details of the conversation with his crew, certainly not the information he had shared with the presumed-dead Jak Moster. He wanted to make sure it was real before that happened. "Any ships in range?"

"None."

He didn't enjoy feeling like a sitting duck. "Extend the scans. Make sure no one's got eyes on us."

"Yes, sir."

He waited a few minutes more, and then pushed himself out of his chair, finding the need for action. Joining Tasiq at the communications console, he busied himself staring at the screens as if he were actually reading something. "Guess I'm being played?" he murmured.

Tasiq shrugged his broad furry shoulders. "Seemed legitimate. All the frequencies checked out." He punched a series of buttons. "This is the place from whence the message originated."

"Well, then, what in Sprechan's name—"

An insistent buzzing cut the captain off. Tasiq's left ear fluttered with interest, and he called the message up onto his monitor.

Bring your transport to the following coordinates.

"Those are the same ones we have now," Temms growled as he reviewed them.

"Not quite. These are off the starboard side about half a mirk." Tasiq glanced up at him. "I guess it's time to lay your *abril* cards on the table."

The captain chuckled at the reference to the game. Tas had only lately been inducted into the ship's card tournaments, the concept of card-playing not a natural part of his culture. He was learning fast. "I guess it is. Have security meet me at the transport bay."

"Yes, sir." Tasiq paged security, and Temms grabbed his comm from the arm of his chair and headed for the door. He stopped in his office to put on his dark blue jacket with the pocket inside that concealed his smallest laser pistol, as well as a scanner and a bottle of good alcohol. He figured Jak deserved it.

In the hatchway outside the slipcraft bay, he was surprised to find Tommy, in uniform, pale but upright, arguing with Nim Williams about who should accompany the captain on this mission.

"I'm perfectly recovered, Williams. No reason for you to have to leave the ship."

"What's going on here?" Temms scowled at his son, but it had no effect.

"I'm going with you. That simple."

"Do you even know where I'm going?"

Tommy looked nonplused for a moment. Then cleared his throat. "It doesn't matter, Captain. It's my duty to protect you wherever you're going. I should be by your side."

Nim fidgeted in his uniform and holstered weapon, trying to get between Tommy and the door. "If you'd like me to wait outside, Captain?"

"I would not." He eyed Tommy. "*You* haven't been out of a sickbed less than twenty-four hours, and Nim is fully briefed on the circumstances of this mission."

"Sir?" Nim's puzzled expression reminded the captain he had been less than forthcoming about this encounter.

Tommy caught the flub and a slow, superior grin came to his lips. "So, captain, you can fill me—us—in on the details as we're crossing to *wherever* we're crossing to." He coughed.

Temms' comm beeped, and a message appeared in text form that Moster was anxious they hadn't appeared yet. He sighed. "Fine, I don't have time to argue with you. But *you*—" He pointed to Tommy. "If you pass out and get useless over there, I'm leaving you right where you fall. Get me? I've got a lot riding on this, and I don't have time for mollycoddling."

"Got you, Captain, sir."

Tommy grinned at Nim, who just rolled his eyes.

"All right, gentlemen, let's go."

Temms led the way into one of the small slipcraft, which seemed a better piece of equipment to use than the tubes, since they didn't know the exact location of the station. The ship launched without difficulty, and Temms proceeded on the heading that had been given them, off the starboard bow.

Tommy leaned forward in his seat behind the pilot's. "So where are we going exactly?"

The captain chewed his lip. "Not sure. Exactly. I'm sure something will let us know when we least…." The vista before him changed in an impossible way, and he trailed off, baffled.

Nim choked on a breath as he apparently spied what the captain had seen. "You mean like when a door suddenly opens in space?"

That was an accurate description. Nothing uncloaked, the station didn't reveal itself, but there was no question that the hatch to the landing bay had slid open in anticipation of their arrival, lights on inside to guide them. It looked just like someone had sliced a hole among the stars, with a station inside. The strangeness of it made him hesitate until Jak's voice buzzed in his ear.

"Get in here, man, before you're spotted!"

Temms quickly punched the accelerator then, skidding a little as he touched down inside the bay. The door slid closed behind them, cutting them off from the rest of the universe.

"Hey, Dad, you're sure this isn't a trap, right? I mean, Captain?"

He secured the ship, and then turned to the two young men. "We're about to find out."

CHAPTER 20

THE hatch opened with a hiss of escaping air.

Nim and Tommy jockeyed for the right to be the first to step out. Nim eventually deferred to Tommy's position as department head. Temms followed them, laser pistol in hand.

Just because we were invited, doesn't mean there's only friends aboard.

The hangar deck they entered contained half a dozen small craft of various sorts. Temms recognized none of them as belonging to anyone specific. No one awaited them on the deck. That surprised him, but no more than the whole venture had. One oddity after another.

"Jak?" he called.

Nim stiffened, turning back to face him. "Jak? Jak Moster? He's here?"

"Apparently."

"We saw the holo that showed his murder. This isn't possible." Nim's face set in a frown. "The Agency wouldn't have proclaimed his death if—"

"If they hadn't intended to deceive us?" He shrugged off Nim's disbelief. "Why should we believe anything those bastards tell us at this point?"

Nim looked as though he was going to speak, but instead his mouth smacked shut. "Yes, sir."

Temms caught Tommy's amused expression, and smiled. "Who knows what wonders we'll find in the next few minutes? All we can do is keep an open mind. Come on, let's see what we can find."

Their slipcraft was brightly lit from overhead, the light source hidden in the ceiling somewhere, its glow following them as they walked toward what he guessed was the door to the main station. The doors slid open without them touching anything, and they stepped into a pristine, surreal corridor with curved white walls, lit by a lavender-blue glow along the ceiling that brightened as they approached each juncture, and then dimmed after they had gone by.

He wasn't the only one who noticed. Both young men stared in curious disbelief as they passed each new technological miracle. Windows to the outside appeared in the walls as they continued along the corridor, revealing the depths of space and stars, and then disappeared into the gray-white blandness again. Their footsteps didn't echo as expected in the empty hallway, but somehow the sound was absorbed in the materials around them so their progress was nearly silent.

They hadn't gone far when a bustle in front of them and light growing progressively nearer brought them to a stop. All three had weapons trained on the blind curve of the hallway ahead, when Jak Moster came into view, looking remarkably well for a dead man, even plump and happy, his balding head shiny under the lights.

"You made it! I apologize for the spy business. As you know, everyone seems to want to get their hands on the place. It behooves us to keep them out. But not you, Temms, not you." He grinned as if his face would split. "We know you're the expert on these items. Your help is just what we need."

How did these rumors get around? "Expert? I don't know about that."

Jak only hesitated a moment. "Don't be modest. I'm sure you'll be able to get things working in no time." He turned and started walking, tossing an invitation to follow over his shoulder.

Nim and Tommy both looked to Temms for orders. He just grinned. "Why not see what's on the table?"

The three followed Jak, hurrying a little to catch up.

"So, Captain Moster, how did you end up here?" Nim asked. "Intel didn't say much about what happened when you got picked up. Ral certainly hasn't come forward."

"Ral hasn't been anywhere around, come to think of it," Temms added.

"Not surprised," Moster said with a smirk. "Little coward's probably turned tail and run. Now here's the control room."

He turned a corner and activated a sliding door that opened to reveal a brightly lit room some fifteen feet square lined with panels full of blinking lights and large buttons with hieroglyphics of the Ancients on them. "So many of these scribbles, and so many I don't understand."

He walked up to one of the panels and pushed a few of the buttons, activating a large monitor in the back of the room. The screen displayed a picture of the *Doubtful*, cruising in space outside the station. "I've figured out a few things. How to work the comm, how to make some of these pretty pictures light up. What we really need is your translation team."

"I have no problem putting my people on this," Temms said. "Do you have a file, some sort of excerpt of introductory material I can send over to them to get started?"

Jak's smile faded for a moment. "Send over? You mean off the station?"

"Most of the equipment with the interface for that language is installed on the ship. I can't just detach it."

Temms didn't add that his most powerful translator was Benzi Quinn, who had been given the ability to understand multiple languages by an Olesian work crew supervisor. Benzi would definitely be on the team he would bring over here to work, no question about that. But the fact Jak hadn't answered the question Nim asked nagged at him.

"So if you had something portable or in electronic form, I could send it directly."

Jak fluttered around the panels, opening and closing drawers, digging in nooks between the machines, searching for something, and eventually came up with a small infostick. "This'll do ye, I think."

Temms took his comm from his pocket and inserted the stick in one end. The file booted up immediately. He glanced over the first few pages, and then transmitted it to the *Doubtful*, with directions for it to be sent immediately to Quinn.

If anyone can figure this out, it'll be him.

"All right, it's sent." He smiled. "So how *did* you get here, Jak?"

"Hmm?" The fat man continued to fiddle with the panels. "Not sure, really. I remember the Agency men snatched us, played their little games, and then I passed out cold." He shuddered. "I was left for dead. I woke up lying on the ground outside Roandock. I was in pretty bad shape, that I'll tell you. Those bastards know how to work someone over. I never spilled, Temms, I swear I didn't. But Ral...."

He paused in his frenetic prowling. "Man would shoot someone cold in a bat of an eye, but he couldn't stand pain. No, sure he couldn't." He sighed.

Tommy eyed Temms, brow furrowed, and then crossed to come face to face Jak. "What did he spill? Something about my dad?"

Jak looked down at the floor, swaying a little. "Wasn't anything they didn't already know, I'm sure."

Tommy grabbed the front of Jak's fancy shirt. "What did he say?"

Nim startled and reached for his weapon. Stunned by his son's vehemence, Temms started across the room, but slowed to a halt when Jak spoke.

"H-He told the Agents that T-Temms was the one who knew the most about—about the artifacts."

Tommy didn't let up, and backed him up against the panel. "And what else?"

Jak raised his hands and covered his face. "That was all I heard, I swear! Just that Temms was the one collecting artifacts!"

Tommy released him, and he staggered sideways, grabbing a countertop to catch his balance.

"So that explains why they've been hounding you," Tommy said, with a growl in Jak's direction. "They don't care about your anti-tariff status. They want the technology of this station and your knowledge of it."

"But I didn't know about it." He eyed Jak. "You're the one we've found here. Who else lives aboard the station? I can't believe you run all this yourself. Someone pick you up off Roandock and bring you?"

The other man straightened his shoulders and got his dignity back in line. "Now look, Temms, you're coming on like I'm your enemy. I don't know how in blazes I got here. I'm just damned thankful to have all my parts and be walking upright. You and me, we both want the same thing, to get this station running like it should be. Guess these Ancients saved my life, so I pretty much owe them. You, too, if all the tales I hear are so." He stepped away from Tommy. "Why don't we get to it?"

"What about other officers?" Temms persisted. "Who else is here?"

Jak shook his head. "Just me. And I may be a lot of things, but heaven save me, I'm no damned engineer." He gestured to the panels. "You're welcome to give it a shot, gentlemen."

Temms batted the possibilities around in his head, finally deciding that his conscience could accept Jak's simple explanation. The Ancients had never explained how they had rocketed the *Doubtful* to this universe. They didn't offer enlightenment on the reason they had allowed Temms to send the *Talon* back through the wormhole, with its trail of destruction following. Why would they make an exception for saving the captain of the *Ramman*?

He shrugged and stepped up to the console nearest him. "None of us are engineers, either, Jak. But we'll see what we can do. Once my team comes up with some more solid plans, I'll deploy a group over here to help you out."

His brisk nod to the two young men he had brought along sent them moving along the panels, studying the Ancients' writing found on the buttons, poking at one, and then another occasionally. Jak stood back, his face lit with hope, his hands anxiously clenched in front of his wide belly.

Despite the time he had worked on the machine that had freed them from the threat of Burko, however, Temms could make no sense of the readouts on the Ancients' equipment. His knowledge of the language was rudimentary at best. He could guess, perhaps even an informed guess, but he was as likely to blow something up as activate the proper sequence. Tommy wore the same confused expression he himself had. Nim moved along the panels, making notes and comparisons, but he didn't seem to come up with anything, either.

When Temms had worked his way all around the control room, he finally had to concede failure.

"This should be a task for those who translated the other artifacts. We could do damage here without any intention. Better to let someone tackle the project who's got some aptitude."

"When can you get someone here?" Jak asked.

It had to be soon. His deadline loomed. Less than two shift-turns left. If the Ancients were to help him against the Agency, he could waste no time. *Quinn better have loaded up the damned files I sent him. Dani's on her feet again, so he can devote his full attention to this assignment.* "It's a priority for me, Jak. Count on someone within the next few hours."

Jak eyed him, a knowing light in his look. "Time's running out."

"You don't have to remind me." Wondering how Jak knew about the Agency deadline, he had to let it go. So many things were happening he couldn't explain. He could only handle the ones he could control.

He let his chest swell with a deep breath, and then let it out, hoping to dislodge the stress that sat like a rock above his heavy heart.

"What about the unit that's missing?" he asked Jak.

The query halted Nim's prowl around the consoles. "Missing?" he echoed.

Jak glanced quickly at the two young men, and then back at Temms. "I—I don't know what you mean."

"The spokesman for the Ancients said that a crucial piece of the station had been stolen."

"By who?" Tommy asked.

Temms shrugged. "They didn't say."

Jak twitched and dug at one of the consoles. "Maybe they didn't know."

This was maddening. He crossed and put his hand on Jak's shoulder. "Jak, have you been working with the Ancients, or haven't you?"

Nim walked up behind the other captain, effectively trapping him in place. "I suggest you answer Captain Rogers' question."

Jak straightened and looked Temms in the eye. "Maybe you are the all-knowing Temms Rogers of the other-universe ship *Doubtful*. I'm not sure what in blazes that gets you when you walk into a bar. What it gets you when you are invited—*invited*—in here is the chance to help those working with the Ancients get this station active so it can reach everyone in the system. I've never claimed I'm anything special, or that I have special powers or privileges. I just found myself here, and I'm counting myself the most fortunate man in this universe to be alive and to be a part of this."

He walked out from behind the console, not even giving Nim a look.

"I've been doing the best I can, all on my own here. I'm just not able to read the hieroglyphics, apparently, because I can't activate it. Please forgive me for troubling you with my pitiful requests for help."

He turned and eyed the three men. "I thought you were the ones who were supposed to help me. If you can't or won't, then I'm sorry I've bothered you."

He paused by the door. "I'll walk you down to the bay."

"That still doesn't answer the question, Jak," Temms growled. "You want us to believe you just showed up here with no evidence of how that happened or how long ago—"

"Three weeks," Jak said.

Tommy came over to join his father. "You've been here for three weeks, all alone."

Jak ran a hand over the console closest to him, its lights blinking and power humming. "I thought I'd done pretty well for a rough mercenary captain without much more training than to keep my damn bird in the air." His jaw jutted out, his shoulders square.

Temms relented. What would he have done under similar circumstances? He didn't have much more experience than that. Could he have gotten basic power on?

"Jak, at least tell me this. Are the Ancients providing you with any information? Anything? A hint of what needs to be done?"

Jak shook his head. "You're getting messages? You're far ahead of me."

"Right." Temms looked at Tommy and Nim. "We need to get a team over here that can really get this mystery deciphered."

Hopefully Benzi had already gotten a head start on the translation. He would find out as soon as they got back. It had to be soon, if he was to enlist the help of the Ancients to get the Agency off his trail.

"Keep at it, Jak. We'll return shortly. Gentlemen, let's head back. We can find out way out."

The three exited the way they had entered. Nim started to ask a question, but Temms cut him off. They shouldn't expect that such an advanced system couldn't monitor them, even if it wasn't operating at full strength. Better to say nothing until they were inside their ship.

"You realize that was total crap, don't you?" Nim burst out, as soon as the hatch was closed. "He couldn't possibly have done this all by himself if he was so ignorant."

Temms nodded. "It did seem a bit hard to swallow. But the Ancients, they work in mysterious ways. We know that, if nothing else, just from how they've led us."

He fired up the slipcraft, and they flew out when the bay door opened. It closed behind them, leaving an unblemished view of space.

"We'll bring our experts. We'll make this work, Nim. Don't worry."

CHAPTER 21

WHEN Dani Jamar walked back into engineering for the first time since her illness, a cheer went up from every man, woman, and alien there, Benzi Quinn's not the least of them. Exhausted from weeks of pulling double shifts to cover for those lost or fighting the virus, he struggled to concentrate on the daily tasks required to run the engine room.

"Thanks, everyone!" Dani gave a shy wave of acknowledgment, pausing for brief hugs or handshakes as she made her way to Benzi's office. Monty met her at the door, throwing his arms around her waist and holding so tight it had to be painful.

Benzi got to his feet. "Hey, snapper, she's just getting out of hospital, huh? You got to be careful with her."

"He's all right," she said. "I'm just so glad to be—" Tears pooled in her eyes as she looked out the window to Halian's regular station. "I can't believe he's gone."

She hugged Monty, who finally let go, and to Benzi's surprise, she reached out to embrace him as well. The unaccustomed gesture, on top of Benzi's drained physical state, stimulated his own sense of loss. Hal might have been a wog, but he was a staunch companion and co-worker. They had nearly lost Dani, too. They had been through a lot together, and now life, as he knew it on the *Doubtful*, would never be the same.

Before he knew it, he was bawling like a baby, clinging to Dani, who was doing the same.

"Pop hurt?"

Monty's frightened voice, along with the hand pulling at Benzi's shirt, brought him back to reality. He coughed to clear his throat, making a business of stepping away from Dani and straightening his shirt. "Pop's fine, snap."

"Sad?"

"Just so, Son. We can be glad Dani's back and still feel sad about—" He shrugged, happy at least that Monty seemed to be coming more into synch with his human emotions. Something that had taken him nearly a year to process correctly. *Maybe the Doc's therapy will make him a whole boy one of these days after all.* "Good catch on your part. Named that feeling right off."

Dani wiped her face and smiled. "You're doing well, Monty."

"Happy you're here." Monty flashed her another smile and wandered away to the artifact table, where he resumed his fiddling.

A few moments of awkward silence left Benzi shifting and shuffling, feeling like his hands had nothing to do. "So you sure you're all right?"

"I'm not one hundred percent, not yet. But I couldn't lay down there any more knowing you were short-handed." She pulled up a chair to the edge of Benzi's desk. He noticed then the dark circles under her eyes, the pinched look of her face. Even her dark hair seemed to have lost its shine. "Brief me on our status."

Benzi called up a list of the latest work orders and shared a quick run-through. "No major repairs or issues aboard ship, other than personnel replacement."

She nodded slowly. "I'm sure sciences filled in while we were out. Anyone you particularly liked, or anyone who had a special aptitude?"

At first, Benzi hesitated to answer. Was she really asking his opinion? Or was this some kind of test? Ever since he had come aboard, he and Dani had shared a stilted relationship, jockeying over control of the department.

His da's voice, the one that always took the negative view, whispered warnings in the back of his head: *No. Who're you kidding, pal? She always had control. Rogers' big joke. Call you chief, but let her keep running everything.*

Right. That.

So was this some game she was playing, waiting to jump on him for making a wrong choice now that he had let his guard down?

"Benzi?" Her face showed concern, eyes narrowed. "Are *you* okay? We can talk about this later, if you want. Probably you should go get some rack time. I've had plenty, myself."

She sounded so genuine. He just couldn't be sure.

"Look," she went on, "we haven't been friends, and that's fine if it makes you more comfortable. But I promised myself, when I realized I might not make it through, that I would try to make this a better team if I made it out the other side. You've worked very hard to keep engineering running, even with your other responsibilities." She glanced out the window to the artifact table. "We've already lost Hal. Let's not lose anyone else."

Why did his throat close up like he was about to cry again? Bleedin' unacceptable, that's what that was. He coughed to clear it.

"Could use a coupla more of them Muuvos. I know they're wogs, but they work real hard."

"Good." She patted his desk. "I'll make a note. Anyone else?"

"That Zandra Cilka's not bad."

The thought of willowy, blonde Zandra, who had been spending a lot of time in engineering lately, cheered him a little. She was the first woman aboard who hadn't dismissed his flirtations out of hand. She really seemed to like and be tolerant of Monty and his issues. Benzi sincerely enjoyed her company.

Wouldn't it be a gift, and a reward for all his hard work, if she was transferred to engineering and they could work together every day? Maybe something would even develop on a more permanent level.

You're dreamin', boyo. No one will ever love your sorry ass.

Shut up, Da. Just shut up.

He focused on Dani's face, the hope she held out to him. Things could change. She believed it. He needed to, also.

"All right, I'll speak to her, too. Thanks for being upfront with me, Benzi. I appreciate your honesty." She shared a tired smile. "Now you should head on out."

Benzi's computer beeped, signaling an incoming assignment. He frowned. He had truly been enamored of that idea of hitting the sack.

"Now what?" he grumbled. Activating the message link, he waited for the download, and then clicked the file open. It revealed a whole diatribe in a language he couldn't read. "Sprechan's blue balls. What is this?"

"Let me see," Dani said. She came around the desk to stand behind him, reading over his shoulder. "Hmm. Some of those markings look like the sets on the artifacts."

"They do, at that." Benzi poked at his keyboard, brought up images of the artifacts already in their possession and set the holos side by side. A definite similarity. He checked the source of the new data. It had come direct from the captain.

"Now where'd he come up with this?" The mystery nagging at him more powerfully than his need for sleep, he buzzed up to the bridge.

Gretta Flan answered, her warm alto tones welcoming the call. "Bridge."

"Yeah, this is Quinn. Let me speak to the Cap, would you?"

"Captain Rogers isn't on the ship at the moment," she replied, her voice gaining a definite chill.

Benzi exchanged puzzled looks with Dani. "Zatso? Where might he be then?"

"He's on assignment. He'll return shortly."

He stared at the intercom, as if it had stung him, and cut the connection. "Well, that's some monster of a mystery then, ain't it? I just wanted to check this out."

"Not sure." Dani clutched at the back of his chair.

He turned to find her eyes closed, her face pale. He jumped up and pulled her chair around the desk, and then sat her in it. "Hey now, don't you be falling down on me, hear? I got no time to cart you back to the infirmary!"

"I'm fine," she protested. "Just haven't been up and around much." She waved off his concern. "Back to the data. Can you read it?"

He eyed her, unsure whether she really meant she was fine, or she was bluffing him.

She'd best not still be contagious. Doc said this was something we all was inoculated against years ago. She's not going to give you anything. Calm down.

He took a shallow breath, not wanting to get her germs. *Just in case.* "Dunno. Let me take a look."

Dialing the viewer to zoom in closer, Benzi studied the calligraphy-like script that lined the pages. He hadn't acquired much book learning, growing up with his alcoholic father and moving from place to place while his father lost job after job, but he had been given a gift by a passing alien.

The memory of Tamala's assault on him burned as long as the flash of memory. The hand the alien had stabbed with his wicked injector ached with the echoes of that recollection.

Gift, my ass. It was a virus, and the effing green wog said so.

Whichever it was, Benzi now had a sort of universal translator built into his very cells. If he kept at it long enough, he would be able to make sense of the scrawls and scratches. The knowledge would seamlessly change, become readable, like a key had been laid over the words.

He studied several pages of the data, but nothing came to him.

"This might take a while. Best leave it to me. Need help to your desk?"

Even as the words left his lips, he couldn't believe he was actually offering to assist her. What was wrong with him? Like as not, she would be after his job duties again in no time. These damned aliens had changed every one of them.

She smiled. "Don't worry about me, Benzi. I'll manage. If you need anything, let me know."

A little unsteady, she walked out of his office and made the slow climb to her desk on the upper level, a place where she could keep an eye on everything below in the engineering department.

Benzi muttered under his breath, something even he didn't really understand, just for the sake of being able to mutter. He wanted to be unhappy about Dani's return, make sarcastic comments about her abilities, even call her out for an open battle. But all he felt was gratitude that she had returned.

Sprechan's playing with me, and that's a fact.

Annoyed with himself, he glanced around to see where Monty had gone. The boy remained at the artifact table, building whatever he had been working on. He seemed less feverish about it today. Maybe that was a good sign.

That left him with the translation. He took his seat again and slowly clicked through the pages, waiting for that moment when the words began to look familiar and then spoke to him.

At some point, he wasn't sure just when, he began to hear his mother's voice in his head, just as he had when the artifacts had been activated to save the ship from the Captain's old enemy a year before.

All is well, my child. Your destiny is at hand.

That sat him up straight.

Remember the good we've accomplished together. You are on the cusp of further discoveries that will change our universe. You, Benzi, will have the power to open the door for us to expand into the many worlds, to bring our promise of a new order to all our children.

"You're what built the machine, right?" he asked in a whisper. "The Ancients?"

Exactly right.

His mother's voice resonated with warmth and love, all that he had missed since she had left his father for that alien lover. He wanted to remain there and bask in that emotion forever.

All you need to do is find the key to that door, my child. Somewhere in these pages, you will find the answer. Once the Odahmeen *is found and installed in our station, we will be able to meet you and reward you properly for all your hard work and devotion.*

He liked the sound of that. He, little Benzi Quinn, would have the power, would receive a reward. Finally someone would appreciate what he did. Oh yes, he liked that.

"Just tell me what I have to do, and I'll get right on it."

The voice whispered to him. He strained to hear it, the world around him slipping from his awareness. He was almost there. Almost there.

Someone shaking his shoulder hard got his attention, dragging it back from what seemed like an interminable tunnel.

"Chief! What's with you? Are you okay?"

"Hmm?" He blinked, disoriented. "What?"

Zandra stood over him, blue eyes a little panicked. She pulled her hand away, and he vaguely noticed her bright pink nail polish, as he tried to get his bearings. He caught a glimpse of Monty in the doorway behind the tall blonde.

Her expression held great concern for him, and she slid onto the chair beside him, taking his hand. "Benz—Chief, I've been calling you for five minutes. You were totally lost in something on the screen."

"I was?" He glanced at the monitor, reassured by the words there. Words now, not some illegible squiggles. He sighed with relief. He had finally hit the right track. "Right. Just working too hard at this translation. What can I do for you?"

She still looked unsure, but she slowly let go of him. "Monty just wanted to get something to eat. If you're busy, I'd be glad to take him down to the galley."

Monty pushed past her, staring deep into Benzi's eyes. "They talk to you. They talk to you, too!" he said, grabbing Benzi's hand excitedly. "Asking for help, yes? Have to find the Shining One!"

"Yes, snap, they talked to me." He smiled at the child's positive enthusiasm, such a change from recent weeks. Again, that reference to "the Shining one" that he had no clue about. "But Pop has to finish reading, all right? Zandra can take you down for some food now. We can talk about it later."

"We'll find her, won't we, Pop? She knows. She knows!"

Wanting to get back to the translation, he just nodded. "Sure we will, snap. Now go eat. Bring me back something, will you?"

The boy was out the door again, sing-songing to himself. Zandra promised to bring him something real special.

"Do you know what he's talking about, chief?"

"I'm not sure, not exactly. Something about the Ancients, though, and those artifacts. We'll get it figured out."

His gaze strayed back to the monitor, and the cascade of words on the page. Before he knew it, he was sucked back in, reading the wisdom of the Ancients. He didn't notice Zandra's fingers brushing his shoulder when she left, or the plate she brought back for him an hour later. He was on a mission now, and he intended to get it done.

CHAPTER 22

LIANG. The time has come.

"Time for what?"

In her bed, half-asleep, Liang looked about for Roddi, whose voice she heard, wanting to see him face to face. He had passed over the veil years ago, before she had taken her first job out of school. He could not truly be here.

It followed, then, that this was another dream. A very realistic one, perhaps, but a dream. As such, it was capable of being directed, or so Roddi had taught. Directing the dream to acquire information might set the ship on a better course than Rogers' blind pursuit of the ephemeral.

In order to take our message to the next level, we must have the control device. Your captain has been charged with the task, and your duty is to assist him in finding it.

In the dream, she was in a space filled with a lukewarm mist. Nothing substantial existed in arm's reach. Her instinct told her that, despite Roddi's warm voice, she was alone.

"You have no more obligation to teach, Master. You are at rest. You have no message to share."

You were always the one who questioned, child. The search for knowledge is admirable.

"Yet you do not search for knowledge."

The knowledge can only be shared with others through the medium of the station. Would you allow them to suffer ignorance because you failed in your responsibility?

The implication that she owed an obligation to nameless others nagged at her. She was a creature of duty, and this is something Roddi knew well. If this wasn't Roddi, then someone or something was using her memories of him to try to control her. The unease this generated started to wake her, but she fought to remain asleep, wanting to have a chance to confront the interloper.

"Who are you? I know you are not my former teacher. If you want my help, you must be truthful."

She had no idea whether the direct assertion would yield the results she wanted. But if the entity was trading on her personality traits, surely it would realize the value of the ruse had passed. Honesty would be the only way to gain her assistance at this time.

The long pause that followed seemed even longer in the misty emptiness.

Child, we are the Ancients who helped rescue your ship from the attack by your captain's enemies. You received our message then, channeled through the device constructed from the collected bits of our history. Do you remember?

The tone of the voice indicated satisfaction, as if sure she did remember.

She thought back to those agitated days, and the joy and relief of the activation of the Ancients' machine. At that time, the contact with the Ancients seemed the answer to a prayer. Thinking of Captain Rogers' interest in this station and the amount of resources he had dedicated to finding it while under a extreme threat from the Agency, she wondered what benefit they might actually gain from this venture.

Better play along.

"What is it I must find?"

The station is locked into the first level of operation at this time to prevent unauthorized exploitation by those who would misuse it. The control unit needed to interface with the station to activate upper stages has been removed and secreted elsewhere. It must be reinstated in order to access these levels.

Liang hit this disclosure like running into a brick wall. It disturbed her in so many ways. If the Ancients had created this station, why would they not still be in control of it? Why did they not know the whereabouts of this control unit? Why did they need common folk to retrieve it? Why could these powerful beings who had changed the lives of so many not help themselves?

She struggled not to let these questions rise to the level of her consciousness that the entity might discover them in her mind. Her semi-conscious state slipping, she hurried on before she woke up and lost contact. "Where do you think I could find it?"

We believe the unit has been hidden under great security by one of the economic factions of your star system.

Economic factions? Dulled by fading sleep, she tried to conjure these names before her. The Agency, of course. The Consortium. The Olesian collective. Jowalt's interplanetary business group. So many. So many.

Don't let time run out, child. The consequences of failure could destroy your captain and his alliance of ships.

Her brain now clicking along into the logic and precision of listing the potential groups, she found her eyes open, staring at her shadowed ceiling. She had lost the connection.

She lay still, processing the conversation. Lucid dreaming was a skill that Roddi taught his students, letting the subconscious work to reveal important messages that conscious thought might be blocking. She had done her best to manipulate that into working here, but she was still mindful that what she had experienced was in fact a dream.

It might be real.

It might not.

In addition to her earlier questions, she wondered whether she was the only one to whom these communications had been made. When the Ancients' machine had been activated, she hadn't been the only one who had received the messages from it. Benzi Quinn had been most closely affected, but also the boy Monty, both working directly with the artifacts in engineering. Several others had, in the post-incident discussions, revealed the communications received during the device's active state.

Including Captain Rogers, who was now seemingly invested in the discovery of the Ancients' station.

That brought her upright, scrambling for her boots.

What were the "consequences" the entity predicted?

Pulling on her uniform, she double-checked her intuitive sense of the interchange. If the Ancients were all-powerful—or at least powerful enough to punch a hole through inter-universal spaces—then how had they lost control of their station? The near-desperation in the voice seeking help seemed to reveal that it wasn't something the Ancients had intended, and they were anxious to recover it.

But why had humans hidden the control device? To protect the Ancients, or to protect themselves from the Ancients?

She left her room and hurried along the gray-carpeted corridor to the captain's office, worried enough to have a meeting with him. The captain had always welcomed her input, even encouraged it. Her concerns might not change the captain's intention, but she couldn't in good conscience let them slide without saying anything.

She rounded the corner to the ladder to head up a deck to command level and came face to face with Nim. He took one look at her and grabbed her arm, keeping her from going up.

"What's happened? You're all flushed and look upset."

When she didn't resist, he led her aside, sliding his arm around her. "Come on, Liang. Something's got you flustered. Share it with me."

She sighed. She had mentioned the dreams before, and Nim had gently teased her willingness to believe in such messages. *But that was before the captain had made his own night visitors public knowledge.*

"I don't know what to do, Nim. I'm concerned about this obsession the captain holds with anything that comes from the Ancients. He's taken them at their word, leading the fate of everyone aboard this vessel onto the edge of a razor."

She chewed her lip. "I trust him. I do. But I don't know if I trust *them*."

He looked down at her, compassion in his eyes, and his hand smoothed her hair away from her face with a lover's touch. "Do you want to tell me what they've said to alarm you? I'm always good for a second opinion."

Feeling validated by his encouraging words, she nodded and then shared with him both what the entity had said and her thoughts about it.

He listened solemnly. Then leaned over to kiss her forehead.

"So many unanswered questions. I know you don't like proceeding that way." He grinned. "My sweet Liang likes to have data and hard facts for her decision-making."

She frowned. "But—"

"Let me finish. I know this is your way, but the captain's way is often to take things on faith. I've heard the stories about how he hired half the people on this ship. I mean, Quinn, for Sprechan's sake. Who else would have done that? He's just that way."

He leaned against the wall, still half-holding her. She wished at that moment they could stay like that forever.

"Besides, Liang, where are you going to get this data to work with? I'm thinking the best source of it will be on the station. Maybe he's right on this one."

Her hope that Nim would back her up a hundred percent fluttered and went out. Was she not seeing something that was obvious to everyone else? She didn't understand.

He leaned close, almost whispering. "I believe in you, love. If your instinct tells you something's wrong, you need to at least bring it to Rogers' attention. Give him the chance to consider all the options. It'll make you both feel better."

She slipped her arms around him and kissed him. Of course he would come up with the right course of action. Speaking her mind would put her heart at ease. The captain had always valued her opinion—perhaps he would take the time to analyze this a little more in depth.

"Thank you, Nim. I will speak to him."

He beamed, lighting her whole world with that smile. "That's my girl. I love you for that determination. You're a feisty little thing." He kissed her, and then released her. "Go on now. See what the captain has to say."

"I'll meet you later so we can talk about it," she promised, and then she grasped the poles of the ladder and climbed up.

The captain responded to her knock with an invitation to enter. She went in, noting Iov's presence, and the schematics and devices that covered the captain's black-surfaced desk. She had no doubt they were all about the station.

The captain was all smiles and enthusiasm. "Liang, I was just about to call you. I want you on this project."

She approached the desk cautiously, giving a nod to the Muuvo. Best to discover exactly what the captain intended before jumping aboard. "What project is that?"

"The re-activation of the station to full power." He gestured at the papers laid out before him, and picked up one of the script-covered pieces, studying it.

Her throat closed for a moment. This was truly the direction their crew was headed, apparently. "Are we sure that is the wisest course, Captain?"

His activity stopped, and he stared at her. "Of course. Why wouldn't it be?"

"The situation doesn't seem strange to you, sir? That after all these years, with all these people and economic powers available to them, that the Ancients' lost station suddenly comes to light when you appear in the vicinity?"

Brow furrowed, Rogers sat down, watching her. "What are you saying, Liang?" He nodded at the chair across from him. "Please, sit. I want to hear your thoughts."

She had been confident about sharing suspicions acquired from a dream with Rogers, aand Nim's support made her more so. Taking the offered chair, she glanced over the items on the desk.

"Captain, am I right in assuming that this station came to your attention in a dream?"

The surprise in his eyes showed her she had guessed correctly.

"I've had dreams, too, sir. Dreams that seemed real, just like a conversation with my instructor Rodolphus. The voice seems so calm, so rational, so real. But I know he's passed on."

"Have the Ancients shared with you the vision for improving life for everyone in this system? The ability to level the playing field economically so that the Agency can't harass everyone? It's an incredible opportunity."

The fervor with which the Captain spoke instilled Liang with a sense of alarm. He sounded like those who had newly discovered the answers of religion. Often they became so excited and energized at their success, that they must tell everyone, even convert them if they could.

She wanted to believe Captain Rogers was more analytical than that. But she knew he also juggled his responsibilities, care for his crew now under attack by the Agency, worries for the alliance he must build with the other captains if they needed to succeed. These were huge concerns about the state of the economic balance he wanted to maintain, for himself, and for all. Above all else, he meant well.

So they appealed to my sense of duty and his benevolent outlook. This was a well-thought out campaign. What else might they have offered? And to whom?

"Have others experienced the dreams?"

His voice took on an annoyed flavor. "They may have. I really didn't ask, Liang. They've come to us asking for assistance. Don't we owe everyone else the chance to experience the help we received from the Ancients?"

Despite the risk of offending him, she believed strongly enough that something wasn't right, so she plunged on. "I think we owe people the chance to know exactly what sort of bargain they're entering. And who they're entering it with."

Iov glanced up, surprised, and then quickly returned to his examination of the artifact in his hands.

"Captain, you've made me your first officer for a reason. I trust it's because you value my opinion. Based on my dreams, and the representations therein, I have serious concerns that we may be misled by an entity that is not honest about their ultimate intentions."

As she spoke, the captain's expression went from irritation to surprise to a puzzled frown. He took a deep breath and picked up a stylus from his desk, holding it over a datapad, poised for notes. "Liang, I know you're not an alarmist. Please, tell me exactly what you mean."

She thought of Nim's encouragement for a moment to strengthen her, and then explained her questions, slowly and completely. "I think we need to be sure who's at risk by cooperation with this entity before we proceed," she added. "A short delay for direct contact surely won't make an issue."

Rogers had stopped writing about halfway through her speech. He sat back in his chair, staring down at his hands in his lap. The minutes passed, and she thought he was considering all she had said, and that she had gotten through to him. When he spoke, it was to the engineer.

"Iov, can I speak privately to Liang?"

"Of course, sir." The Muuvo stood quickly and hesitated. He gave Liang a nod of farewell, and then hurried out.

Liang was not reassured by Iov's dismissal, and what Rogers said next justified her anxiety.

"How?" he asked, tapping his index finger on the table. "How do we contact them?"

She didn't have an answer for him, and she told him so.

"See, that's what's special about this association that we have with the Ancients is just that. It's special. It's magical. These people, whoever they are, have resolved to look out for us. Once we built the device from their building blocks that gave us the power to save ourselves when we rebelled against the Confederation, bringing us here, we showed them that they were making a difference, improving people's lives. They gave us a chance to do it again when we used the artifacts we collected to build the communications device a year ago."

He reached for the cup on the table behind him, and then took a long drink from it. It wasn't lost on Liang that he hadn't offered her one.

"When they contacted me to offer this collaboration, and led me to this place through Jak Moster, I took that as further evidence of their confidence in us as humans who had constructed and accessed the Ancients' own technology. We were *invited*."

"Yes, but—" Had he said *Jak Moster*? How had that ghost aligned itself with this mystery? Surely, there were many more questions than answers. Captain Rogers couldn't be leading them into this storm without considering the lack of information. Could he?

He was not to be deterred, his gaze locked with hers. "These very special beings are giving us the ability to combat the Agency's stranglehold on the system. I have to look beyond just what might benefit or impact our ship and crew and consider what the rest of the people in this system might need. This is my chance to regain the structure of...." He trailed off, and his voice caught.

The structure of what? What was her captain missing? Insight came to her. "You don't have a command system any more. Without the Confederation, you're on your own. It is a difficult adjustment."

He waved her concerns off with a swift gesture. "I don't need the Confederation! They had been corrupted, they had lost their way. They weren't serving the people as they should. The Ancients *want* to serve the people. We can unite with other like-minded beings and make the kind of organization the Confederation should have been."

She nodded slowly. She had worked with him long enough to know when he had reached the point he stopped listening. They had just about arrived there. She stood, facing his desk.

"Captain, I mean no disrespect to you, to your good intentions, or even to the Ancients, who surely have helped us in situations where we needed help desperately. I'm just concerned that these Ancients haven't given us their full agenda. You have a whole crew depending on you, and I simply urge caution."

Rogers stood, too. "I think you've just made my point for me, Liang. The crew depends on me. I'm the one who has to take ultimate responsibility. So I decide. I choose the way that leads to the good outcome for the most people."

He came around the desk, his jaw softening just a little, and he put his hand on her shoulder in his usual fatherly way. "Look, I want you to be comfortable with this. Would you lead the team that goes to the station? That gives you the best possible opportunity to keep an eye on everything. The first time something troubles you, I want you to let me know."

It wasn't much, but her gut told her this was the best chance she was likely to get at this juncture. Maybe he was right. Maybe she was. The next few days would certainly reveal the answer. "I will do that, Captain. I do advise we have a strong complement of security officers, though. Just in case."

"Thank you for taking the assignment, Liang. I'll send along as many security people as I can spare. I promise."

His smile warmed his eyes, and for a moment, she felt their old connection solidly in place. That was the important part. If they couldn't work together, neither of them, or perhaps any of the crew, would get through this next few days, facing the Agency ultimatum and the curious station discovery. The strength of that bond among them would be the only thing to save them all.

CHAPTER 23

LIANG piloted the cargo shuttle *Phoenix* over to the station, and Rogers experienced the strange phenomenon again as the open bay door revealed the interior of the landing platform there in otherwise unsullied space. So strange, almost magical. Like everything else they had discovered about the Ancients' creation.

The faces of the others who had come with them reflected the same amazement. Benzi had volunteered from engineering, fresh from his review of the data Rogers had sent earlier. He insisted on bringing Monty with him, since the boy had in the last days worked himself into a frenzy over the artifacts on the ship. Temms had tried to dissuade him from taking the child, but Benzi reminded him of the boy's gift with the alien devices. He couldn't really argue with that.

Benzi had brought along Uri and Iov as well, since much of the work on the station would involve deciphering what was needed to activate the more sophisticated levels of the technology there.

Tommy and Nim represented the security team, since Aronka was near her delivery, and Tabio was beside himself trying to keep Rey occupied and under control. *Funny how we thought human babies were such handfuls, but at least when they went into a crib they couldn't just slither through the slats and vanish.*

In consideration of their little family growing and prospering, he let them remain, secluded, in their quarters on the lower deck near engineering. There would be plenty of time for them to participate once the station was fully activated.

All in all, Temms felt like he had a real team set to come aboard and decipher the panels. The missing controller, whatever it was, would surely become apparent, since Jak hadn't been helpful about its existence or location. Once they had a real idea of what they needed, it would be easier to search for it on the planets below.

The shuttle bumped to a stop. "We're ready," Liang announced, flipping the controls to their off position.

"All right, folk, grab up your kits and let's go," Benzi ordered.

Temms stayed out of the way as Iov and Uri stacked plastic cartons of equipment and tools on two wheeled carts. Monty stood off to the side, singing to himself in an off-tone, repetitive, non-rhythmic manner that ran chills right up Temms' spine. Tommy opened the hatch, and then the four of them rolled the carts off onto the bay floor.

"Jak said to start on level three," Temms said. "Most of the main computer equipment's there."

Tommy hesitated, but Temms waved him on. "Go with them. Jak's probably got some questions about information security. Nim and I can show Liang around."

"Yes, sir." Tommy flashed him a smile, and then climbed into the lift with the engineers and their cargo.

"What would you like to see, Liang? The Ancients don't have anything to hide from us here."

She studied the walls as they continued along the corridor, occasionally touching a panel with her small fingers. "The power runs so quietly," she said.

He cocked his head, listening. He hadn't really considered that point, but she was right. A hushed hum vibrated through his feet, indicating the station was alive, but, unlike his ship, the mechanism that kept the station running was near-silent. "Do you want to see the control room? Even though this whole station is about four times larger than the ship, it runs on a power source about the size of our main engine."

"How can you say that?" she asked, walking beside him. The sound of their boots on the polished floor was absorbed into the very walls. "Have you ever seen the station? It's always been cloaked, hasn't it?"

Nim continued to walk behind them, but there was no doubt from his intent posture that he was hanging on every word. Temms' irritation grew as Liang continued to prod his enthusiasm for this project.

Couldn't she just have faith?

In the next moment, the answer came to him. It would be difficult for her to take anything at face value after what she had been through. Liang was a cautious young woman, coming from a life of insecurity. She had been an orphan alone in the world, and then betrayed by her first captain, and a slave to Oke Runyon before Temms had rescued her. She had a reason to see the dark side of a cloud before she could perceive any silver lining. He just had to show her whatever she needed to see to overcome that pessimism and prove he was on the right track.

Once she accepted the goodwill of the Ancients, she would be just as passionate about the collaboration as the others. By the hells, if Benzi Quinn could get excited about such an endeavor, there was hope for anyone!

"It has to remain cloaked. If the Agency got their hands on this, who knows what damage they could cause?"

He diverted her response by taking a ladder passage to the floor below, where Jak had earlier showed him the station's power plant. Seeing was believing, as the saying went. He didn't understand the science that went into the beating heart of the station, but he had spent enough time in engine rooms in ships of the Confederation to recognize this was a level advanced well above any of them. The workings moved behind their pristine panels with a minimum of sound, activated by panels of buttons on a single console. Level one hummed along without their interference. All they had to do was figure out how to activate the upper levels.

She dutifully followed him, and while she and Nim studied the machinery, speaking softly to each other, he checked in with his team back on the ship, who were continuing to actively search for the potential of any missing parts either as part of their own collection of artifacts or on any of the nearby planets.

The Ancient who had spoken to Temms in the night visits had been quite specific that the key to activating the station's powers was contained in a piece of equipment that was missing. Liang had added the Ancients' revelation that some "faction" had hidden it. But which one? And where?

The only thing he knew for sure was that his time was running out. The Agency's deadline counted off in four hours. Benzi had assured him that he had a grip on the basics of the data he had reviewed. If the team could somehow jump-start the station's defensive mechanism without the missing part, he believed they would be able to handle an Agency attack. The full release of the upper levels of power could be added. He just needed this one thing.

After what the Agency had done, he didn't intend to simply disclose the location of the station, or make any other cooperative move. If he could, he would find a way to make the defensive capabilities take out the Agency's top ships, just to make his point. He didn't intend to play *nice* any more.

Liang came around the side of the power plant. "Has Captain Moster invited any of the other captains in your group to come aboard?"

"I don't think so."

Nim turned from his examination of the machine in front of him. "You don't find that strange? If you're all in this together?"

Liang studied him, curiosity flashing in her dark eyes, as she awaited his response.

Called on his decision, he admitted to himself that he hadn't considered that fact at all. Jak had termed him the "expert." He had just accepted that designation. But in the face of Liang's skepticism, it sounded full of hubris to say so.

"I think others will come as we get systems online. We had more experience with the Ancients' artifacts. So we were invited first."

Nim snorted with derision. "I doubt many of them have the courage to even venture here, especially with the Agency practically hanging right off its bow."

Liang chewed her lip a moment, and then crossed her arms. "We surely are fortunate to be held in such high regard by the Ancients, as to get all their blessings and assistance."

His fading excitement couldn't blind him to the underlying cynicism in her voice. But he was determined it would not dull his drive. "Come, you can ask Jak your questions in person."

"I will welcome that," she said.

They went up the near-silent lift to the control center. When the door opened, they found Benzi and the others already busy at work, their machinery hooked up to the Ancients' equipment. From the conversation he picked up when they walked in, he could guess Quinn and Iov were interfacing some sort of translation device. Uri and Monty hurried around in a seeming random pattern, making notes from different sections of buttons.

Temms studied Liang, waiting to see if the spark of curiosity would finally win her over. Sure enough, once she checked in with Iov, reviewing some of the work they had already translated, she seemed fascinated.

Good. She'll warm up to this, and once she's invested, everything will be fine.

Jak Moster bustled over to greet Liang, practically bubbling over with eagerness. "I'm so glad you're here, Ms. Chen. Your reputation as a dedicated officer precedes you."

Rogers caught the sardonic look Quinn threw Liang's way, but the engineer didn't miss a beat with his hands. He was extraordinarily motivated for this venture, almost suspiciously so. An echo of Liang's caution wafted down through Temms' mind like a hint of smoke. If her theory was correct, and the Ancients had approached each of them with the offer of something dear to their hearts as reward, what might they have promised Quinn?

The sad thing was, he couldn't afford to care right now. He needed this station to help him.

Back on the ship, the team had sent out feelers to all the usual sources, looking for a trail of the missing part the Ancients claimed was the key to elevating the station's functioning. Liang's compiled list of organizations had been contacted. Some had replied. Some hadn't. Most indicated they had no idea what Rogers was talking about. Some implied that it would be best to leave them out of anything that implicated the wrath of the Agency.

He walked over to join Quinn. "Is there anything I can do?" he asked. "I'm not expert, but I've got a pair of hands. Come on, Jak. You, too."

The seven of them put in the better part of a watch, gaining bits of ground, losing others. It seemed that the station didn't intend to give up its secrets, especially when it came to the threshold question of how to power it up to the next level, until Monty dug into a bag of artifacts he had carried along with him, and plugged several into various ports in the control room. Small bursts of power spiked and fell. Then repeated in a cyclic pattern that showed they had tapped into something new.

"Good work, snapper!" Quinn said, patting the kid on the back. "Now let's see what this mother can do." He and the other engineers started a concerted effort around the circuits Monty had bumped up, Liang keeping track of all the changes in a central location, coordinating the effort. Jak scurried from person to person like a starving rodent, gathering data and parts to pass to the others. The energy felt positive, as if progress was being made. He could leave the work in the hands of those who were working on it.

Temms checked his chrono. Two hours left. Time to get back to the ship and prepare for his meeting with the Agency. He wished his team luck, bid them farewell and took the shuttle back.

* * *

FEELING satisfied with the progress they had made, Temms returned to the *Doubtful*, retreating to his office to formulate his final rejection to the Agency.

He steeped a cup of sharp-flavored rooibos tea, considering his conversation with Liang. Perhaps he had won her over, or at least set her on the path to seeing things the right way. If she, Benzi and the others worked together, he was confident they would come up with a solution to the station's issues, and he would be able to access the power of the station to repel the Agency.

Once he showed he could have a real impact against the tyranny of the Agency, the other mercenary captains would join the fight. C. T. had left a message they were on stand-by. All he had to do was call.

A shudder ran through the *Doubtful* at the same time the proximity alarm went off. Kai's raised voice came over the intercom calling for battle stations. The ship shook again, and Temms realized they were under fire. He sprinted for the bridge.

"What in blazes is going on?"

"We're under attack, sir!" Kai vacated the captain's chair and moved to the tactical console. "Agency ships!"

Stunned, Temms took the chair and dialed up the outside view on his monitor. Sure enough, half a dozen of the silent black Agency cruisers held sky, two directly around his ship, and the others in proximity to where he had left the Ancients' station. "Get them on the comm, now."

Tasiq tapped in commands, and then waited. "I'm not getting a response, Captain."

The station's cloak flickered, revealing a glimpse of the outside, which was an oddly iridescent copper-tinged color. A few more flickers, and then the station came solidly into view. The appearance gripped Temms' throat with confusion.

Was the station coming on line to fend off attackers? Was that all it needed?

More importantly, his people were there, stranded now that the Agency was between him and the station. How would he get them out?

Fear for their safety thickened his throat, and he choked over his words. "C-Comm them again."

"Yes, sir." Tasiq did his magic with the board, and this time, Temms' monitor screen lit up. Agent Delcin appeared there, his bureaucratic smirk firmly in place.

"Ah, Captain Rogers. Almost in time for the deadline we set. I suppose we can assume you didn't intend to meet it."

Not much point in arguing that, even if he wanted to. The consequences weren't that important any more. "You've located the station, I see."

"We must thank you for leading us to it," Delcin said, leaning back in his chair as if he didn't have a care in the world. "We'll be sure to give you the credit in our next press release."

The statement burned Rogers, as they had surely intended.

"I want my people back," he said, trying to keep a confrontational edge from his voice. Delcin felt superior enough. No need to egg him on.

"You've got people on the station?" Delcin's expression was the very essence of innocence. "We're investigating now. Anyone we find will be taken into custody until their motives and allegiances are determined." He leaned closer to the screen. "We can't have random rabble-rousers running loose, you know. Bad for business."

Knowing what this could mean, what it had meant in the past to others who now laid dead, his anguish threatened to shake his reason. Not only had the Agency gained access to the station and exposed it for all to see, they were taking the low road regarding his people. He could imagine the burgeoning size of Liang's "I told you so."

"My people have nothing to do with this, Delcin! Release them to me."

"When we're past the threat."

Now they were being ridiculous. "Five officers and a child? How big a threat to you anticipate them to be?"

"Not them, Captain. You and your agitators. We'll hold these people to make sure you don't try something stupid."

A wave of frustration curled around the bridge. Everyone seated there suddenly sat a little straighter, more tense, and most of them looked to him to do something to solve this problem.

Problem is, I don't have an answer right now. I need time to think.

And I need Liang here, by my side. Tommy, too.

But they weren't here, they were *there*, trapped behind the Agency's blockade.

"This isn't the end of this, Delcin," he growled, and he gestured to Tas to cut the feed.

As soon as the screen went black, he hit the ship-wide intercom.

"This is the captain. All senior officers to my office immediately. Repeat, all senior officers to my office. Now!"

He got up from his chair, passing by the communications station on his way out. "You hear anything else, you let me know."

His head spinning, he walked off the bridge and down the hall to his office, wishing he could get his hands on a real solution. Or Delcin's smarmy pencil neck.

CHAPTER 24

"THEY'RE here!" Monty squealed, and threw himself into an open console panel, hiding from view.

"What are you doing, snap?" Benzi pulled himself out from under the panel he was working on, something in the child's panic setting off his own alarms. "Who's here?"

Could it be the Ancients? Had his team gotten the attention of these absentee landlords, and they had decided to make a visit to help out? That would surely be the stroke of luck that had eluded him all day.

All the *Doubtful* officers' comms went off at the same time, broadcasting an alarm, and then shut off in mid-alert. Nim took off running down the hall.

Liang frowned, trying to get them back. "The signal is being jammed."

"Let me see that." Benzi scowled and reached for her comm, ignoring his own. The Ice Princess had probably hit the off button, and was too proud to admit her mistake.

She hesitated but finally slapped her comm into his outstretched palm.

Jak Moster poked his head into the control room.

"What's going on?" she snapped.

"They found us."

"Who?"

"The Agency. I don't know how. Temms must have—" His anxious expression turned into a scowl. "If he told them where we are, the Ancients will have their revenge on him!"

"Don't be a flophead," Benzi interjected. "Cap may be a lot of things, but a traitor ain't one. If anything, they probably followed your bleedin signal in." He fiddled with Liang's transmitter for several minutes, but couldn't find a thing wrong with it. "Like as not, they're the one's what's jamming us, too." He checked his own, finding the same result.

Tommy Rogers came barreling into the control center, a laser pistol in each hand. "Agency's boarding! How the hell did they find out?"

"We don't know," Liang said. "More importantly, can we keep them out?" She studied the nearest piece of equipment they had brought from the ship, still in mid-translation.

Iov flexed his thick arms and lifted a computer onto the nearest flat surface, where it was closer to eye level. "Perhaps. The protocols are not finished running, but we may have enough interface at least to block off this room."

"Do it," she said.

Tommy looked around the room. "Where's Williams?" he asked, voice tight.

Liang glanced up. Then left and right. "He was here before the alarms went off."

"Fine. I'll see if I can get eyes on the situation," Tommy said, and he was gone again.

Benzi took the moment to sling himself under the heavy metal console with Monty. The child was curled up in a fetal position, fretfully humming to himself in an off-key, loud tone that hit Benzi like the scratch of nails on a chalkboard. He shook the boy's shoulder.

"C'mon, snap, maybe that caterwauling keeps you from thinking about bad things, but it's keeping me from thinking anything useful! Please, knock it off, will ya?"

But he just kept on.

"Mr. Quinn, I need you," Liang said. "You must set up the station's inner defenses to keep the Agents out of the core."

He slid out, and then eyed her like she had just sprung two more sets of arms. "Right. And when I'm done with that, maybe I can snap my fingers and get us all a nice *jumma* steak dinner too. Shall I now?"

At the same time the impertinent words were coming from his mouth, he was already in transit to the machine, trying to decide if he had enough language skills to give such an order to the station. Surely some system existed to close off corridors in the event of a disaster of some kind. As long as they didn't cut themselves off from life support and the Agency didn't either, they would be all right until the Cap could figure out how to bust them free.

She glowered, but didn't reprimand him. Guess she knew he was their only hope.

Yep, and you'd best be nice to me if you want me to save your frozen ass.

A small voice in his head acknowledged his own need for salvation, too. He had better save Monty and all of them while he was at it. He paused for a moment, almost prayer-like, trying to reconnect with whatever intelligence he had encountered in his office when he uploaded the file the Cap had sent. Surely someone who had spoken to him so sweet didn't want the Agency prods to get to him, right?

He sincerely hoped so, anyway.

He set his fingers on what they determined to be the main keyboard and closed his eyes. *Point me in the right direction, mama.*

The muscles in his hands twitched, and then moved without his volition. "That's it," he murmured, opening his eyes, absorbing the keys he touched, letting the language of the hieroglyphs implant itself in his brain. As time passed, he took over control of the data entry, interfaced with the machine itself.

His consciousness expanding, as it had when he and the machine unified a year before, he could sense the Agents and their minions moving through the corridors toward the place where they hid. With a few flicks of his fingers, he activated defensive force fields in mid-corridors to block their progress.

Liang watched over his shoulder. He noticed she pulled away, almost afraid to touch him. Monty, though, now he came out from his hidey-hole and snuggled right up into Benzi's lap. It was a really awkward trick, since he had started that pre-puberty growth spurt and was much too big for such things. But Benzi accommodated him, because he knew the boy had some real magic with the Ancients' tools.

"Come on, snapper, let's chase 'em away."

Monty nodded and laid his hands on top of Benzi's.

Even though the scanners wouldn't work, none of them, Benzi didn't need them to detect the Agency ships. Several hung off just off the exterior of the station, between it and the *Doubtful*, which was just on the perimeter of Benzi's sensing limits.

"They're going to shoot, Pop!"

"Who will shoot?" Liang demanded.

"The black ships. They're going to shoot home!" With a despairing wail, he cowered under Benzi's chin.

"Snapper, come on. Stop a minute, you're—"

The boy's thrashing knocked Benzi away from the keys, and he lost contact with his vision. He bodily lifted Monty off his lap and handed him to Liang. "He wants a hug, you hug him. I gotta work here."

By the time he got his hands back to the computer, though, he had lost whatever momentum he had. He tried again and again, but it was no use. The connection was severed.

Jak ran out into the hall, and then returned, Tommy on his heels. "Whatever you did, you've kept them out. They've tried to penetrate the core a dozen different ways, but they can't get in here."

Iov slumped onto a console, his face contorted in his expression of sorrow. "But we cannot escape, either." He glanced at his brother, Uri. "Nev will be beside himself."

Uri's eyes widened, and his jaw hung open, as he assimilated the news. "We have each other, each with skills carefully polished in a way that could save us. Captain Rogers will not allow us to be taken."

Benzi got up, annoyed that his efforts had been derailed. "Yeah, well good luck to him. Agency's got him outgunned at the moment, with all those ships."

Liang frowned. "How many? We could not see what you saw."

Benzi laid out the situation, while Tommy growled at each new fact. "Cap might have a few superior weapons, but in sheer numbers, Agency's got him by the short hairs. And I'm betting they're using the fact we're here against him. He don't know they can't get to us."

She sighed and sat down in the nearest chair.

"So we're trapped, and help's not coming."

CHAPTER 25

WITH all the comm units useless, Liang tried to focus on some avenue that wouldn't lead to a wall, but couldn't come up with one. Monty continued to cling to her, practically in her lap, keeping her from moving freely around the control room, keening in a particularly minor tone that dug nails into her spine.

"We're going to have to find something to occupy him," she said softly.

"I could take him to get a snack," Uri said. "If there is a galley within the rooms we are able to access."

"Sure. Just down the hall," Jak said, pointing.

Iov frowned. "You should not go alone. In case the enemy breaks through." He eyed Tommy, as if to suggest the security man should go with them, but the captain's son was clearly not budging from his position by the door to the control room.

"I can do it, brother," Uri said, standing a little taller.

When Liang peeled Monty away from her, intending to hand him to Uri, the boy began flailing his arms and screaming.

Benzi Quinn got out of his chair and came over, grabbing the boy by his shoulders. "Monty!" he yelled.

The first time he said it, he startled everyone on the deck, including the boy, who only cried louder.

But he repeated the boy's name, a little more quietly each time. While it did nothing to soothe Liang's nerves, Monty's distress seemed to fade with each repetition. When he finally quieted to the point he could listen, Quinn told him that Uri would get him something to eat, if he would go with the other boy. Monty sniffled some more, still exhibiting some nervous tics, but finally he walked out with Uri.

Setting the issue of what to do with Monty aside, Liang sized up her situation, stuck behind enemy lines with two men who had never particularly liked or trusted her. *What a blessing.*

The voice of irony dripping over her, she couldn't even fool herself.

But what bothered her now, more so as the minutes passed, was Nim's absence. He had disappeared at the very first alert, and he hadn't come back.

"Did you see Nim when you were out on patrol?" she asked Tommy.

"I didn't." The captain's son frowned. "Did he call in?"

He pulled his comm units from his belt and paged Nim.

No response.

If he had run into one of the Agency men, he could be hurt, or even dead. Liang couldn't forget the images from the holos they had seen.

She checked to see she had her weapon. "I'm going to look for him."

"Do you want me to go?" Tommy asked.

"No. We need someone here to make sure the crew is safe while they're finishing the work the captain ordered. Don't let those perimeter shields down."

"Yes, ma'am," Tommy said, with only a hint of sarcasm. Liang brushed it off and left the room, heading down the main corridor toward the bay where they had parked the shuttle.

She took out her comm unit and keyed the mike, testing to see if she could pick up any signal at all once she left the control room. At first, all she got was static. Then a faint voice, male. A second male voice. She turned down the left hall, took several steps, and the voices faded out. She turned around and headed down the corridor to the right, finding the voices getting stronger. When she realized one of the parties was Nim, she nearly broke in to the conversation, but hesitated a moment.

"I'm trying to short-circuit the shield on the angled hall, sir, but the usual methods aren't working."

Liang slowed down, her heart clenching tight. What was Nim saying?

"We don't have time to waste, Williams. *You* don't have time to waste. Rogers' team got this up and working. There should be no reason why you can't take it down."

It couldn't be true.

She stopped, thinking she should go back and get Tommy. But something drove her on. She had to know.

Praying she had misunderstood, she rounded a corner and found Nim prying at a control box with a screwdriver. Just past him, on the other side of the transparent force field, stood four men in full Agency uniform, armed with dangerous-looking, large firearms.

"If I didn't know better," she said, her voice choked, "I'd think you were trying to let the Agents in to penetrate the station's core."

Nim froze, and then looked over his shoulder at her. "Liang, love. Why couldn't you have stayed back to play with the science types, just this once?"

Her blood boiling, she took a step closer. "Is that it? Is that what you're doing?" She studied the array of tools he had dumped on the floor.

He stared at her. "You don't understand—"

His comm unit buzzed angrily, and the man closest to the barrier banged dully on the other side. "Williams, get the shield down *now*."

Liang inched closer, nearly in arm's reach. "You can't do this, Nim. You can't betray everything we're working for."

His jaw set. "Like you said, how can a society who can't even operate its own machinery deserve to be the ruling group in the sector?"

Sick at his betrayal, she balled up her emotions and shoved them deep into her belly. She came at him, fists flying. He stabbed at the mechanism one more time and then turned, screwdriver in hand, to fend off her attack. Avoiding the sharp edges of the tool, she grabbed his wrist and pulled hard enough to swing him past her into the wall.

The screwdriver flew out of his hand when his elbow hit. He slid halfway down to the floor before he recovered himself, and then shoved off, coming at her with his right arm extended. When she ducked to avoid his grab at her throat, he snatched her hair with his left hand and dropped to the floor. She had no choice but to go down with him, but she went kicking, trying to get at some vulnerable point, but he held her off. He yanked her on top of him, holding her around the neck, and then flipped them both over so he pinned her to the floor.

"Sorry I have to do this, love. You should have minded your own business."

She caught a glimpse of his arm raised. Holding the pistol by the barrel, he brought the butt down on her head.

Everything went black.

CHAPTER 26

"SO where's the Ice Princess gotten off to?" Benzi muttered.

He studied Jak Moster, who flitted around the control room, checking a panel here, a monitor there. He didn't seem as concerned or upset, even about the Agency's arrival, considering his level of interest in the secrecy of the station before Rogers and his team had arrived.

What was wrong with this picture?

"She went looking for Williams." Tommy scowled. "She should have been back by now." He pulled out his comm unit and tried to get a signal, but all he got was static.

"Come here'n see this," Benzi said, gesturing to his monitor.

Tommy pulled his chair close, eyeing the screen like he understood any of the scrolling data that passed across it.

"Do you think this Moster's character's on the up and up?" Benzi asked him, softly, so that Jak couldn't hear. "Don't his behavior seem odd to you?"

"What do you mean?" Tommy asked.

Benzi cocked his head, taking in the entire room without actually looking at it. "Seems not too worried for a man about to lose all his secrets." He smirked. "Course maybe he thinks my superior skills got us well covered."

Tommy glanced at Moster. "We've kept the Agency on the outside for now, though. That's what we need to do. I just wish we could get through to the *Doubtful* and let them know what's happening."

"I expect the Cap will figure out how to deal with them."

Iov joined them, looking at the screen as though he was totally dedicated to translating what was there. "From what the crew has said, the captain seems to be able to conjure miracles sometimes." His smile faded. "But hard to imagine how it would be possible here. The Agency is quite determined."

"The Captain won't let them stay," Tommy interjected.

"Guess all we have in our favor is that the station ain't complete without that piece. If we can't make it work, with all our experience working with the artifacts, sure as Sprechan's ass, those Agency clowns can't do it neither."

"All the same, our orders are to keep the place secure," Tommy said.

Jak cleared his throat, inched his way closer to them, pausing at last just behind Quinn's chair. "So, what are you going to do?"

Benzi got to his feet. What was Jak up to? Why was he so focused on what the *Doubtful* crew was doing? "What do you propose?"

"Me? You all are the experts here." Jak's wide smile was that of a disinterested and insincere host, not someone whose life was on the line. "I'll defer to your good advice."

Benzi stepped away from the console, taking a walk around the control room, studying each panel, with its blinking lights and input ports. By the time he came back to Jak again, he had a theory. He didn't like it. But he had one.

"Who are you?" he asked.

"Who am I?" Jak stepped back and laughed. "What do you mean, who am I? Jak Moster."

Tommy got slowly to his feet, weapon in hand now trained on Moster.

"Don't think I'm sure, pal. I ain't never met you, that I do know. All I know is the Cap told me to come here and help you figure this out. I'm doing my part, but I don't see you doing much to translate anything." He watched the fat man, whose expression struggled between laughter and irritation.

"Don't be ridiculous! Come on, we need to continue working on the defense systems," Jak said, pushing past him to tap at the console where Benzi had been working. "You were doing so nicely."

Tommy glared at Benzi across the top of Moster's broad back.

"He don't talk much like a captain, does he?" Quinn said slowly.

"For someone who's lived here for weeks all by himself with no one to help him," Iov weighed in, "he's certainly not very conversant with the very life support that's sustained him."

Before Benzi could respond, Uri and Monty returned, an empty box in hand. Monty's tear-streaked face revealed only despair.

"Nothing to eat in the galley," Uri said. "Looks like it was cleaned out months ago."

That raised Benzi's eyebrow. Why would Jak have casually sent the boys there for food if he knew the cupboard was empty? Either he hadn't been there or he didn't need to keep sustenance on hand.

"Answer the question, pal," Tommy said, his voice tight. "Who are you?"

Jak looked from one to the other of them. "We thought—"

His form slowly dissolved from that of the jolly, rotund missing captain to an amoeba-like column of muted yellow light. Monty squealed and grabbed onto Benzi. Iov and Uri came immediately to Tommy's side, completing the circle around him.

Jak's voice came into Benzi's head. No, not his voice any longer, but the voice of his mother.

We believed it would be easier for you, as humans, to work alongside another of your kind, rather than interact with us. Your captain had an established camaraderie with this man that lent itself well to gaining his cooperation. We had such hopes for a collaboration, your crew and ourselves, to share our message with the cosmos. But you failed to bring the station to the next level of power, despite our best efforts. Perhaps we were wrong to choose you.

"Look here, Mama," he muttered. "Ain't like I can pull gold out of a coal pit, now can I?"

The spokesman for the Ancients continued. *These Agents seem quite resourceful. We shall take your Captain's reservations about them into consideration, of course, but it is possible they will succeed where you failed.*

"They are quite treacherous and have only their own glory to guide them," Tommy warned.

The hour grows late. What we need is the station, fully operational. We can take measures to deal with the Agents, should they not follow the orders they are given.

"What will you do with us? Return us to the ship?"

The light pulsed and faded for a moment, as if in thought.

No. We shall interface more productively with the Agents if they believe they are in control. It is unfortunate this leaves you as their prisoners.

A beam of light shot out from the column to one of the panels. Quinn ran over to see what was happening, dragging the clinging Monty with him.

"Bleedin' Sprechan's hangnail, he's scotched the outer shields. We're done for!"

Tommy aimed at the light-thing, and pulled the trigger, but nothing happened. Heavy footsteps came down the hall toward them. Despite his oh-so-reasonable mother's voice reassuring him that they would not be harmed and all would be well, Benzi didn't believe a damned word of it. They were screwed.

Four large, broad-shouldered Agency guards marched into the control room, one of them carrying an unconscious Liang, and Nim Williams bringing up the rear.

Tommy shot at the closest guard, but again, the weapon didn't fire. Benzi shoved Uri and Monty behind one of the large free-standing consoles, catching a glimpse of Iov picking up a heavy wrench. The Muuvo held it slightly behind his back, ready for whatever came next.

Man after my own heart.

Benzi snatched up a soldering gun, flicking the switch on to let it heat up. If regular weapons wouldn't work, there were still the old fashioned kind.

The guard dumped Liang into a chair, standing close behind her. "Drop your weapon," he said to Tommy.

"Get the hell off the station!" Tommy retorted.

The guard held his gun to Liang's head. "Now."

Tommy hesitated, before tossing aside the gun.

Nim stepped out from behind the guards. He still had his laser pistol, and he raised it in Tommy's direction. It took several seconds for Benzi's analytical mind to process the scene, but finally the realization sunk in.

"Sprechan's balls, man! Are you working for the Agency?" Another second, another analysis. "You let the bleeding internal force-fields down?"

"Traitor," Iov muttered.

Studying the slumped Liang, Benzi's dislike of the "Ice Princess" slowly melted away, and he wondered how badly this member of his crew was hurt. "And what about Liang? Is she dead? Are you just another Agency murderer?"

Tommy bristled. His facial expression flared into anger. Benzi could imagine his hands throttling Nim's neck quite handily.

"She's not dead," was all Nim said.

"Silence!" barked the guard with the most 'fruit salad' on his collar. He turned to the Ancient. "We claim this station and all its technology for Tuon Donn, the Agency and its subdivisions."

It was disturbing to Benzi to hear his mother's soft laugh emanate from the glowing thing. Under his breath, he ordered the boys to stay put, and then he inched closer to Iov. The two together could make a stronger attack. All they needed was a distraction.

"I believe you are mistaken to think you could own this base," the Ancient said.

Guard #1 pulled back so suddenly, an odd expression on his face, Benzi had to wonder who "spoke" to him. Clearly someone more frightening than Benzi's mother. Knowing the Ancients came to each person as a different authority figure from their past, he could only guess it was someone who had an iron fist. *Maybe Tuon Donn himself, the scary old bastard.*

"We will permit you to assist us. You will be rewarded for success. Failure will bring you nothing."

Liang moaned and tried to sit up, stealing the attention of everyone on deck. Nim started to go to her, but Tommy growled a warning, ignoring the weapon of the guard that held Liang. He hurried to her side.

"Liang, talk to me. Are you hurt?"

"My head," she murmured. As she came fully awake, she stiffened and tried to stand up. "Nim! Stop him!"

"Now," Benzi whispered to Iov.

As one, they launched themselves at the low console nearby, landing feet first on top of it, and then using that leverage to send themselves the few meters toward the guards. Iov swung the wrench at the head of one, connecting with an ugly thunk, and the guard went down. Benzi's legs weren't as strong as the Muuvo, and he hit the floor instead of his target, but he quickly jammed the soldering gun's hot end right into his man's midsection.

Iov got in a second hit before the remaining guard slammed him into a console and knocked him unconscious.

Benzi's target let out an agonized yell and batted him aside. When he would have stomped Benzi with his heavy boots, the Ancient intervened, enveloping Benzi in some sort of protective glowy case that fit closely around his body, immobilizing him.

"No. We need this one. He can read the signs."

Struggling, Benzi found himself hyperventilating. Was there air? Would he suffocate in there? He had thought they were bad off before, but now?

Surprised Monty hadn't thrown a fit, he turned to see that Uri physically restrained the kid, whispering in his ear. *Good thing them Muuvos were strong, right?* Iov lay on the floor. Tommy had pulled Liang away, setting her up in a chair on the far side of the room, both of them glaring at Nim.

The Agency guys, the ones who weren't clutching some injured part of their bodies, continued to argue with the Ancient. The words were muffled through this thing that held Benzi, and frankly he didn't care what they said. Both were just a different form of devil as far as he was concerned.

And they're keeping me from my chance at glory and riches with all that clap-trap. I had most of the code worked out. I think I even got a bead on that missing piece, down there on Terza, and I know who's got it tucked away. That boy Monty's smarter than most give him credit for.

But right now, I believe I'll be keeping that news to myself. Until I know I'm gonna get the chance to follow it on my own.

Then his gaze fell on Nim Williams, who stood apart from all the others, his attention fixed on Liang. It occurred to Benzi that in this last interchange, Nim hadn't raised his gun or taken a pop at anyone. He just stood there, looking a little defeated. *So what's his game? Is he in or out? And what's with him and the Princess?*

He struggled some more with the case, realizing that it wasn't entirely solid, so he definitely had air. But he wasn't going anywhere until the Ancient released him.

Yeah, I had it right. We're screwed.

CHAPTER 27

TEMMS Rogers slouched in his chair on the tiny observation deck down the hall from his office, staring out at the stars, his heart feeling very much like that cold, empty void.

He had purposely chosen this place because he could relax and be alone. But it had the added advantage of being pointed in the opposite direction from the Ancients' station and the small fleet of Agency ships surrounding it. The evidence of his failure.

He needed this space to think. He had met with his team, and for the better part of a day-turn shift, they had brainstormed, but none of the answers they generated could be immediately put into action. Tasiq and Gretta were double-teaming the communications issue, but they hadn't been able to get through to any of his staff on the station. They were thoroughly cut off.

And here I sit, unable to help them do a damned thing.

He poured two fingers of the brandy C. T. had left him last time he was aboard, and set the bottle on the floor next to his chair. A drink would take the edge off, and with his anxiety dulled, he hoped he would be able to think more clearly. But in his head, Connie nagged at him about the futility of drinking at a time like this.

You've taken my son from me, and now you've lost him, you bastard. What are you doing about it? Clouding your brain with that swill? Just like you. You never did look far enough ahead to have any real plans. And now Tommy's gone.

Temms drained the glass and tossed it across the room. It broke against the thick glass of the ceiling-to-floor port.

What in the hells was he doing?

Why hadn't he *seen* it?

He shook his head, hoping it would clear, and then sat forward, forehead in his hands. Beating himself up wouldn't help now. He needed action. He needed a plan. A *real* plan.

What did he have going for him?

His team on the station was a solid one. Tommy, Nim, Liang, Benzi and the Muuvos, they had all be planning some way to get out of Agency custody. Jak Moster surely had a backup strategy. Likely he was regretting inviting Temms aboard, but he wouldn't have exposed himself without some alternative, an escape pod, a secret exit. The *Doubtful's* bridge crew would monitor space all around the suspected location of the station for any sign of flight.

On the outside, he had his loose association of mercenary pilots, but he knew they would probably split along courage lines. Those who valued their independence more than their skins would stand with him. He might be able to rally some assistance off the planets, too.

But not the Consortium. The one group that might actually be able to help me.

"We'll do it without them," he murmured, first as a promise to himself. "We'll do it without them." A little stronger, more convincing, this time. The third time he made it a promise to his first officer, his engineers and his son.

"We'll do it without them."

He stood, ready to head back to his office, when his comm buzzed.

"Rogers."

"Captain, Agent Delcin wants to speak to you."

A shudder ran through Temms. *It better not be bad news. It better not.* He moved close to the glass, where he felt almost a part of the starry cosmos before him.

"Patch him through."

"Yes, sir."

The patch had the advantage of not being visual, only audio. It was all he could handle at the moment. He cleared his throat before he keyed the message.

"Rogers."

"Captain, there's been an accident on the station."

Temms ran the words through his head six, seven, eight times, not willing to accept them. He forced a response between his lips. "Do you need our assistance?"

Delcin's polite laugh hit the captain as hard as a punch. "Hardly."

Why had he called then?

Temms' exhausted brain waged war with the burst of adrenaline that rushed through him. Was Delcin's intention just to taunt him? No question the Agency would be so cruel to someone who had defied them.

Delcin spun out the moment for longer than Temms could stand it. The captain gripped the back of his chair tightly, so tight his fingertips tore a hole in its covering. Finally the Agent spoke.

"One of your crew members got out of control and he had to be put down. We couldn't handle him here. I'll send a transport over to bring him to you. Delcin out."

A rush of chilled blood ran through Temms as he stared at the dead comm. Was someone dead? Had to be put down. Out of control and he had to be put down.

What the hell had Tommy done?

Pretty much sober now, he called the infirmary.

"Okalani, I need you to meet me at the slip bay. Bring your kit."

He cut her off before she could pry. Then he alerted Kai to keep tactical at full alert. "I don't want them to be able to sneeze when they come near us without us knowing."

Reassured that any approach would be micromanaged, he summoned Tabio in stealth mode. Steeling himself, he made his way to the bay.

Okalani joined him there, dressed in her casual clothes. She caught his eye on her and shared a sheepish smile. "I didn't take time to get formally dressed. I hope that's all right."

"Fine," he said, staring at the heavy doors.

"Who's coming, Temms?"

He couldn't give her a response. She set her medical bag down and stepped in front of him, looking up into his eyes. "Are you all right? What can I do for you?"

His breath came out in a shuddering whistle. "This one's all on me, Lani. It's why I can't offer you anything, as much as I might like to." He took her shoulders in his hand and gently moved her back to his side. "I've got to be single-minded about taking care of this ship and her crew, or else I make mistakes. I'm so sorry."

Her eyes filled with tears, and she just stared at him.

"I'm sorry," he said again.

She seemed to shake herself. Then she swiped at her eyes and stood straight, looking ahead. "So am I, Te—Captain."

The silence stretched between them until it was painful. It ended when a scraping came on the far side of the lock. Kai signaled that the Agency ship had docked. Temms shut down his feelings and went to release the hatch.

The transport's hatch opened and an armed man came through, followed by two others carrying a stretcher with a body on it. Okalani gasped. The men set the stretcher down and returned to their ship without saying a word. The hatches closed.

Temms hunkered down next to the stretcher, studying the young face. He didn't see any bruises or signs of mistreatment, other than a thickly-bandaged hand.

"Monty?" he said softly.

The boy suddenly sat up, screaming in some language Temms didn't understand. He grabbed onto Temms, trembling so hard he nearly shook the captain off his feet.

Okalani knelt on the other side and scanned the boy. "He's in good health. Looks like he sliced his hand open, but otherwise he's fine." She reached out to pat the child's back.

When she made contact, the child screamed even louder and then bolted for the hatch. Temms barely had time to clamp a hand on his ankle and take him down before he opened the hatch, leaving them open to dead space. When Monty hit the floor, he pulled himself into a fetal position and shut down.

They waited several long minutes for him to come back to them, but it became clear he had gone to another place.

Temms and Okalani exchanged looks steeped in emotion.

"It wasn't Tommy," she whispered.

He nodded slowly. "It wasn't Tommy."

The realization prodded him into forward progress once again. He scooped the boy into his arms and carried him to the infirmary, Okalani following behind. He left the child in her care, and then made his way back to the bridge.

There would be no sleep tonight. The Agency held his people, and they occupied the station the Ancients had entrusted to him. This couldn't stand.

Before the end of the next shift, he had to come up with a plan.

Then he would rescue his team.

And the Agency would pay.

THE END

AUTHOR

Lyndi Alexander always dreamed of faraway worlds and interesting alien contacts. She lives in a skewed dimension in northwest Pennsylvania, a single mother of two children on the autism spectrum, finding that every day feels a lot like first contact with a new species.

PUBLICATIONS INCLUDE:

Clan Elves of the Bitterroot series (Fantasy):
THE ELF QUEEN (Book I)
THE ELF CHILD (Book II)
THE ELF MAGE (Book III)
THE ELF GUARDIAN (Book IV)

Horizon Crossover series (Science Fiction):
HORIZON SHIFT (Book I)
HORIZON STRIFE (Book II)
HORIZON DYNASTY (Book III)

Science Fiction novels:
TRIAD

CHARACTERS AND TERMS

ON THE SHIP *DOUBTFUL*:
Temms Rogers: Captain
Kai Windthorp: Helm Officer
Dani Jamar (D): Chief Engineer
Halian (Hal): Assistant Engineer
Riviera Brown: Junior Tactical Officer; becomes Science Officer
Heath Montgomery: Former Ship's Doctor, now deceased
Thomas (Tommy) Rogers: Captain's son; junior security man; becomes chief of security
Tasiq: Communications Officer
Benzi Quinn: Engineer Assistant with the title of Chief
Okalani Boro: Runaway Bride; Ship's Doctor
Lavan: Medical orderly
Iov: Muuvo who has joined with his brothers, engineering staff
Nev: Iov's brother, works in medical as an orderly and tech
Uri: Iov's brother, works in engineering as a junior officer
Zandra Cilka: Recruited from the Sol Aeris school, sciences officer
Shiro Vered: Sciences officer, often cross-assigned to medical
Gretta Flan: Communications officer from Sol Aeris
Nim William: Security officer from Sol Aeris

FAMILY MEMBERS:
Connie: Temms' ex-wife
Alex and Linz: Temms' twins, left behind
Geoffrey: Okalani's jilted fiancé

ON MARRIEL:
Oke Runyon: Saloon owner
Liang Chao Chen: Waitress; becomes Doubtful navigator
Kevan Ankho: Liang's former captain on the Palva

ON ROANDOCK:
Jowalt Edward: Merchant, parts dealer

SOL AERIS TECHNICAL SCHOOL:
Mosk: Personnel officer

ON LENNOR:
Rez, Malka, Zareb, Jonel and Karn: Lenci priests and officials; old priestess and her helpers

ON TERZA (Home of the Consortium):
Rabal Klin: Minister Hace; minor functionary
The Boy: Abandoned by the Olesians on the ship; taken on by Quinn like a son (Monty)

ON PERPETRA:
The Lumina: Young girl in training for her eventual ruler-ship
Prince Arlen: Grandfather of the Lumina, important man in both Cartesian culture and economic structure
Aronka and Tabio: Shape-shifting security guards of the Bellonan species who transferred to the Doubtful

AGENCY OFFICERS:
Delcin: Agency Officer
Indro: Agency Officer
Eldin: Agency Officer
Tuon Donn: Overseer of the Agents with a cruel reputation

OTHERS:
Rodolphus (Roddi): Liang's former instructor

SPECIAL TERMS:
Lok cha: Deadly drug
Kiritan: Cave dwellers on Lennor, fierce feline predators
Sprechan: Deity of sorts
Abril: Card game
Odahmeen: Ancient device separated from their invisible station, preventing it from activating to a higher level
Jumma: A large bovine animal

www.ingramcontent.com/pod-product-compliance
Lightning Source LLC
Chambersburg PA
CBHW022121170626
46808CB00002B/797